Pregnant?

A tentative excitement wrestled with her apprehension. One moment, joy held sway. In the next, anxiety had gained the upper hand. An unplanned pregnancy? She gulped. It sounded so irresponsible. Irresponsible people shouldn't be allowed to raise children.

She hugged her handbag. No. She hadn't been irresponsible. She and Alex had taken precautions. It was just that sometimes— obviously—accidents happened.

She frowned over that word—*accident*. Her baby wasn't an accident. It was lovely—a miracle.

Alex wouldn't think their baby lovely. He'd definitely think it was an accident—a mistake. She closed her eyes. It was pointless telling herself now that she was through with thinking about Alex. They were having a baby. That changed everything.

MICHELLE DOUGLAS
The Secretary's Secret

TORONTO NEW YORK LONDON
AMSTERDAM PARIS SYDNEY HAMBURG
STOCKHOLM ATHENS TOKYO MILAN MADRID
PRAGUE WARSAW BUDAPEST AUCKLAND

Recycling programs
for this product may
not exist in your area.

ISBN-13: 978-0-373-17774-5

THE SECRETARY'S SECRET

First North American Publication 2011

www.Harlequin.com

Printed in U.S.A.

At the age of eight, **Michelle Douglas** was asked what she wanted to be when she grew up. She answered, "A writer." Years later, she read an article about romance writing and thought, *Ooh, that'll be fun.* She was right. When she's not writing, she can usually be found with her nose buried in a book. She is currently enrolled in an English master's program for the sole purpose of indulging her reading and writing habits further. She lives in a leafy suburb of Newcastle, on Australia's east coast, with her own romantic hero—husband, Greg, who is the inspiration behind all her happy endings. Michelle would love you to visit her at her website, www.michelle-douglas.com.

Books by Michelle Douglas:

CHRISTMAS AT CANDLEBARK FARM
THE CATTLEMAN, THE BABY AND ME

Other titles by this author available in ebook

To my grandparents,
Bunny and Beryl Snaddon,
with love and thanks for all those
wonderful summer holidays!

PROLOGUE

THE intercom on Kit's desk buzzed and instantly her heart hammered up into her throat.

'If you'd come through now, Ms Mercer.'

Kit's toes curled at the rich black-coffee voice. Her heart lurched back into her chest to thump out a loud tattoo. When she leant forward to depress a button, her finger was surprisingly steady given what was happening to the rest of her body. 'Certainly, sir.'

Her finger might be steady but the huskiness of her voice was more Marilyn Monroe than sensible, strait-laced secretary. It should appall her, belying as it did her attempts to match her employer's professional formality, but it didn't. His formality made her lips twitch.

That formality delighted her; energized her.

She seized her shorthand pad and tried to stop herself from racing straight into his office. Cool. Calm. Collected. Her smile widened. No hope of that whatsoever!

Still, she paused at the door to smooth a hand down her skirt. Adjusted her shirt. Undid her top button. Her fingers lingered at her throat, remembering…

Heat rose up through her. Anticipation fired along each and every one of her nerve endings.

She did her best to dispel the images that rose up through her. She didn't want to appear like a trembly, needy teenager in the throes of her first crush. She wanted to look like a woman in control, like a woman who knew what she wanted. She wanted to look seductive.

She bit her lip to rein in a smile. What she wanted was for Alex to take one look at her, grin that sexy grin of his and take her in his arms. Kiss her. To sweep the polished surface of his enormous desk clear and make love to her.

Her legs grew languid, her breasts pushed against the crisp cotton of her shirt. She gulped in a steadying breath. *Stop it!* Alex had indicated how he wanted to play this. And last night had proved just how well she and Alex played together. She smiled again. She couldn't seem to stop smiling. They'd play it Alex's way this morning. Tonight they'd—

No. There'd be plenty of time to think about that later.

She lifted a hand to check her neat, businesslike bun and then, swallowing back her excitement, she pushed through the door, chin held high. 'Good morning, sir.' She made her voice brisk.

'Take a seat, Ms Mercer.' He nodded to her shorthand pad. 'You won't need that.'

She placed it on the desk in front of her then very carefully folded her hands together in her lap and waited for a cue. She loved that oh-so-serious look on his face, couldn't wait until he said something sexy and husky in that masculine burr of his. She couldn't wait to take the pins from her hair, to shake it out till it fell around her shoulders in a newly washed cloud, and to then walk around this enormous desk of his. No, not walk—sashay. She'd sashay slowly around to him like the siren she was starting to think she was.

The siren she'd become in his arms.

Once she was face to face with him she'd slide up to sit on his desk. She'd cross one leg over the other, making sure the action hitched up her skirt to reveal the silky tops of her stockings, held in place by a lacy suspender belt the colour of coffee cream. Then she'd undo the buttons on her blouse, her fingers lingering over each one, until she'd revealed breasts practically spilling out of the tiniest wisp of lace imaginable in matching coffee cream.

And she wanted to watch his face while she did it.

She zeroed in on his face now, holding her breath and waiting for her cue, aching to play out that fantasy. His lips opened, lean and firm, and the breath hitched in her throat. Thick, hot yearning tumbled through her.

This man was all she'd ever dreamed of and more. Last night had revealed that to her in undeniable glory. They'd moved together with an accord that had been more than physical. Last night had been the most wonderful night of her life. When Alex's passion and gentleness and generosity as a lover had touched her soul.

Words emerged from those lean lips of his. Kit relished their black-coffee timbre, savoured their resonance, and drew in deep breaths of his dark malt scent. She'd caught a trace of that scent on her sheets this morning. She'd placed those sheets in the washing machine with a faint sense of regret before she'd left for work. She'd cheered herself with the thought that it'd take more than laundry powder and water to wash those memories away. Of course, there were all those new memories they'd make too and—

'Kit?'

The staccato whip of Alex's voice hauled her out of her thoughts. It hit her then that she'd been so busy relishing and savouring that she hadn't taken in a single word he'd said. 'I'm sorry.' She glanced down the length of her nose at him in as cheeky a fashion as she dared. 'I was a million miles away.'

It took an effort of will to hold back her smile.

He let out a breath and glared. She blinked and sat back with a frown. What on earth had she missed? Had something gone awry with the Dawson deal? The deal Alex had been chasing for the last eight months. The deal that they'd clinched and then in their elation...

He leant forward and his glare intensified. 'Do I have your full attention?'

She swallowed. 'Yes.'

'I was saying that what happened last night was unfortunate and regrettable.'

Each word was clipped out with precision. Short, sharp, unmistakable. Barbs, bayonets, slashing at her. Kit flinched and half lifted an arm as if to ward them off.

No!

His mouth grew straighter, grimmer. 'I'm sure you agree.'

Unfortunate? Regrettable? Her stomach tumbled in sudden confusion. How could he say that? Last night had been wonderful.

'I beg your pardon?' She prayed he wouldn't repeat it. She prayed she'd heard him wrong.

He held her gaze. Unlike her, he didn't flinch. He looked cold, hard...alien. 'This time I believe you heard what I said. And that you understand exactly what I mean.'

The room spun. She gripped the edge of her chair and hung on tight, praying her sense of balance would return and halt this sensation of endless freefall.

A denial sprang to her lips as the room and Alex swam back into her line of sight. *He was wrong!*

She released her iron grip on her chair. 'Let me get this right.' Her hands trembled. Perspiration gathered beneath the collar of her shirt, beneath the underwire of her bra. 'You're saying you wish last night never happened?' The perfectly monitored air-conditioned air chilled the skin at her throat, at her nape, of her bare-but-for-nylons legs. She resisted the urge to chafe her arms. 'That you...*regret* last night?'

'That's exactly what I'm saying.'

She stared into his face—cold, hard, the face of a stranger—and greyness leached in at the edges of her consciousness, swamping her joy, blanketing her in a thick fog that her mind struggled to think through.

The air conditioning chilled a layer of ice around her heart, numbed her brain and robbed her eyes and mouth of all natural moisture. She'd never realized before how much she hated air conditioning.

Beyond Alex, through the floor-to-ceiling plate-glass window, morning light glinted off the white sails of the Sydney Opera House with an absurd gaiety that was reflected in a thousand different points of light in the water of the harbour.

How had she read this man, this situation, so wrong? She lifted her hands to massage her temples. She wasn't some doe-eyed schoolgirl easily seduced.

No hot-blooded woman would deny Alex's all-male magnetism, and last night she had most definitely been hot-blooded.

But not doe-eyed!

A demon of panic clawed at her throat. *This wasn't how it was supposed to end.* He couldn't deny this connection that existed between them.

She dragged her gaze from the sight of the harbour, alive with yachts and ferries, to the man on the other side of the desk. He leaned towards her and she forgot to breathe. What would he do if she leaned across the table too and pressed her lips to his? She'd bet her bottom dollar it'd drive the deep freeze from his eyes.

He jerked back, folded his arms. His face became even

more stony and unreadable. 'It can never happen again.'
He must've registered her shock because he added, 'Not
that I'm denying it was enjoyable, pleasurable.'

His eyes darkened, as if in memory of the amazing
things they'd done together last night, and everything inside her clenched.

'Nevertheless, it cannot happen again.'

'Why not?' The question slipped out of her like the air
from a slowly deflating party balloon. She knew it wasn't
what he'd wanted her to say. She hitched up her chin. Why
shouldn't she ask? It wasn't as if she had anything to lose.

Except a good job.

Well, okay, it was a great job.

And maybe some pride.

She pushed her shoulders back. Who gave two hoots
about pride at a time like this? And good jobs were a dime
a dozen to someone with her qualifications. 'Why not?'
she repeated, louder this time.

'Because you're the best damn secretary I've ever had!'
He slammed his hand down on the desk, the force half
spinning him in his chair. He glared at the wall to her left.
'And I don't want to ruin a great working relationship by
sleeping with you.'

Why were men so afraid to call it making love? She
stared at him, willing him to meet her eye, silently urg-
ing him to unsay his words and to put this right. When he
didn't she said, 'From memory, there wasn't much sleeping involved.'

She cleared her throat and leaned towards him. 'And, for
the record, I don't think it was unfortunate and I certainly
don't regret it.' *So there.* All his square-jawed, broad-
shouldered, tight-buttocked masculinity could take that!

One of his superb shoulders shifted, its power barely
disguised by the impeccable cut of his suit. She recalled

the feel of the firm flesh of those shoulders beneath her fingertips, the crisp whorls of hair on his chest, and her mouth went dry. She recalled the silky hardness of him and her body's delight at his touch with a clarity that made her insides tremble. She would never forget her soul's delight at a night of lovemaking that had blown her apart and put her back together again both at the same time.

He pushed out of his chair. 'It can't happen again.'

Oh, yes, it could. And so, *so* easily.

He shoved his hands into his pockets and pinned her to the spot with his dark, frigid eyes. 'And it won't happen again, Katherine, because I don't do long-term, I don't do marriage and babies, and I certainly don't do happy families.'

He'd called her Kit last night, not Katherine.

'And if I continue to sleep with you you're going to eventually realize I'm telling you the truth and that you can't change me. Then you'll get hurt and angry, there'll be ugly scenes and recriminations and then you'll up and leave without giving me so much as a week's notice.'

It took a moment for the actuality of his words to sink in. When they did, her jaw slackened. He had to be joking, right? These couldn't be his actual thought processes.

His dark hair glinted almost black to the Opera House's white. She stared at him and her stomach billowed with an inexplicable emptiness as the scales finally fell from her eyes. For the last eleven months she'd been in love with a lump of rock.

Alex Hallam was a lump of rock.

Not something light and porous like limestone either, but something hard and impenetrable.

Like granite.

CHAPTER ONE

'KATHERINE MERCER?'

The receptionist glanced up expectantly as Kit pushed through the door. Kit nodded and tried to find a smile. 'Yes, that's right.'

'Dr Maybury is almost running on time. If you'd take a seat, she shouldn't be too much longer.'

Kit smiled her thanks. The surgery had managed to fit her in for the last appointment of the day and the waiting room was deserted.

She sat. She crossed her legs and bounced her foot. She glanced at her watch. She shifted on her seat, glanced around the waiting room, glanced at her watch again and finally seized a magazine. It wasn't that doctors' surgeries made her nervous. It was just—

The magazine fell open to a celebrity wedding spread with the bride and groom in a variety of cheesy but romantic poses—arms wrapped around each other, staring deep into each other's eyes, feeding each other wedding cake. For a moment all Kit could do was stare. And then she slapped it shut and shoved it back into the magazine rack.

All that giddy happiness.

She closed her eyes and pulled in a breath. It was three months almost to the day since Alex had so brutally ended their… She could hardly call it a relationship, and still there were images—like the ones in that magazine—snatches of conversation, a scent, that could hurtle her back in time and remind her of her stupidity. Remind her of the ridiculous dreams she'd woven about a man who hadn't been worth a single one of them. Reminded her of her appallingly bad judgement.

It was crazy too because she and Alex had hardly spent any time together during these last three months. He'd flown to the Brisbane headquarters of Hallam Enterprises the day after his no-nonsense rejection of her and he'd remained there for six weeks. He'd only been back in Sydney for two days when she'd found herself given the fancy title of Project Manager and moved to another department two floors down.

She'd welcomed that change, but… She uncrossed her right leg to cross her left leg instead. She bounced her left foot. She let out a breath and stared up at the ceiling. Was she becoming too hard to please? Was that it? It was just… The project she was heading up was one that had previously excited her. She should be raring to go, eager, engaged. But she traipsed into her office each day as if she had nothing more interesting to do than filing and data entry.

Why?

She was the one who'd urged Alex to pursue the book deal McBride's Proprietary Press had offered him over four months ago. And she was the one who'd hoped she'd get the chance to head the project up.

Midway through last year, she'd written a profile on Alex for a book titled *Australia's Most Successful Entrepreneurs*. That had led to a whole chapter in another book called *Advice From Australia's CEOs*. Now McBride's were launching a new series called *From Go to Whoa*, and they wanted a book with Alex's name on the cover detailing a land development project from its earliest stages through to the final development. The title they'd floated was *Commercial Land Development: from Scrubland to Shopping Mall*. Kit had already substituted *shopping mall* with *sports resort*.

She should *love* what she was doing.

Her eyes narrowed. Had she lost her zest for life because a man had disappointed her? *Pathetic!*

She slapped her hands down onto her knees and glared at the wall opposite. From now on, whenever thoughts of Alex surfaced she was ousting them out of her head pronto. It was time she started having fun again.

She brightened marginally. At least for the next three weeks she didn't have to worry about running into Alex, didn't have to steel herself for accidental meetings in the corridors at work, there wouldn't even be the risk of catching an unexpected glimpse of him in the distance. A week ago he'd left for a month-long odyssey to Africa. Rumour had it that he was doing some kind of aid work.

Not that he struck her as the aid worker type.

She uncrossed her legs. Re-crossed them. Well, okay, maybe he had three and a half months ago, but not since—

No. She wasn't doing that any more. She was through thinking about Alex, through trying to work him out. 'Enough,' she muttered under her breath. She had more important things to think about.

Like the reason she was sitting in her doctor's waiting room at ten to five on a Friday afternoon.

She gripped her hands together. If this was what she thought it was, then…

She squared her shoulders. She'd get through it. Adjustments would be necessary, but it wouldn't be the end of the world. This could be taken care of.

'Ms Mercer?'

Kit jerked around at the receptionist's voice and tried to smile. Would she have to have a needle? She didn't like needles.

Of course you'll have to have a needle. The doctor will have to take blood.

The receptionist smiled kindly, as if she sensed Kit's nervousness. 'This way; the doctor is ready for you.'

Dr Maybury was middle-aged, kind and unfailingly practical. 'Now, Kit, it's been a while. What seems to be the problem?'

Kit pulled a face. No sense in beating about the bush. 'I'm worried I might have diabetes.' She pulled in a deep breath and quickly detailed her incredible thirst, her endless trips to the bathroom—especially at night. 'The thing is, though, that sometimes there's nothing, just a drop or two. And I'm so tired all the time. And hungry.'

'Dizziness? Nausea?'

'I've felt faint a couple of times.'

'Blurriness of vision?'

Kit shook her head.

'Well, let's not waste any more time.' Dr Maybury handed Kit a cup. 'We'll test your urine.'

Ten minutes later, Dr Maybury turned to her and folded her arms. 'I'm pleased to say you are not diabetic.'

Kit slumped in relief. 'Oh, that is good news! The thought of having to give myself daily insulin injections…' She shuddered.

'Kit, you're not diabetic, but you are pregnant.'

Kit blinked. She shook her head. 'What did you just say?'

The doctor repeated it.

She shook her head again. 'But…' Her chest tightened, her stomach cramped. 'But I can't be! I just had my period.'

'Some women maintain their period throughout their entire pregnancy.'

Kit could only stare. 'Heavens,' she found herself murmuring, 'how unfair is that?'

Dr Maybury smiled and Kit shook herself again. 'No, you don't understand. I can't be pregnant. I haven't had morning sickness and…and my breasts haven't been sore…and…I mean you have to have sex to get pregnant and I haven't had sex in, like, forever!'

She hadn't had sex since that magical night with Alex. Her mouth went dry. 'Except… One night…'

'One night is all it takes.'

'But…but that was three months ago.' She couldn't have been pregnant for three months and not known.

Could she?

She thrust out her arm. 'Please, do a blood test or…or something!'

'I will take blood and send it off to the lab to make a hundred per cent certain. But, Kit, the pregnancy test I just used is roughly ninety-seven per cent accurate. I can do an internal examination to eliminate that final three per cent of doubt if it will put your mind at rest.'

Kit nodded mutely.

After the internal exam and when Kit was dressed again, she forced herself to meet the doctor's eyes. 'Well?'

'There is not a doubt in my mind that you are pregnant. And, like you say, I'd put you at about three months. The results of the blood test will give us a better indication of your due date.'

She could tell the doctor the exact date of conception, only she didn't have the heart to.

'Kit, what do you want to do?'

She couldn't be pregnant. She just couldn't be. Alex, he'd…

She closed her eyes.

'If you'd prefer a termination, we can't leave it too much longer.'

Her eyes flew open.

'Do you want children, Kit?'

'Yes.' The word croaked out of her.

But she'd wanted to do it the right way—married, with a divine husband whom she adored and who adored her in return, and with a mortgage on a cute little house and… and planned. Not like this!

'You're twenty-eight. How much longer did you mean to leave it?'

She didn't have an answer for that. Through the fog of her shock, though, one thing started to become increasingly clear. She swallowed, twisted her hands together. 'I don't want to terminate my pregnancy.'

Her doctor smiled.

The answering smile that rose up through her suddenly froze. 'Oh, but I've been drinking tea first thing in the morning and again at lunchtime and—'

'You don't have to give up caffeine altogether. Are you exceeding more than three cups a day?'

'No.'

'Then that's okay. Alcohol?'

She winced. 'I usually have a glass on Friday and Saturday nights.'

'Any alcoholic binges in the last three months?'

'No.'

'Then there's nothing to worry about.'

'I haven't been taking folate.'

'You can start that today.'

Kit leaned forward. 'You really think my baby is okay?' She couldn't stand the thought that she might have somehow hurt her unborn child.

The doctor patted her hand. 'Kit, you are a healthy young woman. There's absolutely no reason to suppose your baby isn't healthy too.'

She let the doctor's words reassure her. Finally, that smile built up through her again. 'I'm really pregnant?' she whispered.

'You really are.'

'But that's lovely news.'

Alex Hallam wouldn't think it was lovely news.

The doctor laughed. 'Congratulations, Kit.'

Who cared what Alex Hallam thought? She was through thinking about him, remember? She beamed back at the doctor. 'Thank you.'

Pregnant!

Kit left the surgery and turned in the direction of the train station. When she arrived there she couldn't remember a single step of her journey.

Pregnant? A tentative excitement wrestled with her apprehension. One moment joy held sway. In the next, anxiety had gained the upper hand. An unplanned pregnancy? She gulped. It sounded so irresponsible. Irresponsible people shouldn't be allowed to raise children.

She hugged her handbag. No. She hadn't been irresponsible. She and Alex had taken precautions. It was just that sometimes, obviously, accidents happened.

She frowned over that word—*accident*. Her baby wasn't an accident. It was lovely, a miracle.

Alex wouldn't think their baby lovely. He'd definitely think it was an accident, a mistake. She closed her eyes. It was pointless telling herself now that she was through with thinking about Alex. They were having a baby. That changed everything.

Her hand moved to her abdomen, cradled it. She imagined the tiny life inside and her mouth went dry. How on earth would Alex react when she told him the news?

I don't do long-term, I don't do marriage and babies, and I certainly don't do happy families.

Nausea swirled through her. Her eyes stung. Would Alex reject their child as ruthlessly and dispassionately as he had rejected her? Her throat thickened and then closed over completely. When her train arrived she boarded it like an automaton, found a window seat and concentrated on her breathing.

A baby deserved a mother *and* a father. Had she robbed her child of that chance because she'd misjudged Alex so badly? She should pay for that mistake, not her baby. She'd messed everything up and now her baby would pay the price.

The rush and clatter of an oncoming train as it sped past her window made her flinch and then sit up suddenly straighter. What was she doing? She couldn't control how Alex would react, but she could control how she dealt with the news. She had a miracle growing inside her and she wanted this baby with every atom of her being. The weight pressing down on her shoulders melted away. A smile built up inside her.

She was having a baby!

The minute Kit entered her apartment she let out a whoop, shrugged her arms out of her coat and threw it up in the air. She was going to have a baby! And then she danced around the coffee table before falling onto the sofa and grinning at the blank screen of her television, at her sound system, at the magazines scattered on the coffee table.

She was going to be a mother.

Her hands formed a protective cocoon across her abdomen. 'I'm going to be the best mother that ever walked the earth,' she vowed, making the promise out loud to her unborn child.

And Alex *I-don't-do-happy-families* Hallam?

She lifted her chin and pushed all thoughts of Alex aside for a moment. He was out of contact for the next three weeks and she wasn't going to let thoughts of him darken her day or dim her joy. He might not do happy families but she did!

She reached for the phone and dialled her mother's number in Brisbane. Today was for joy. 'Mum, I have some wonderful news.'

'Ooh, do tell, darling.'

She heard her mother's grin down the line. It widened hers. 'Mum, I'm going to have a baby!'

She held the phone away from her ear as her mother squealed her delight. 'Darling, I'm so happy for you! I can't wait to be a grandma. When are you due?'

Kit counted six months off on her fingers. Was that how one did it? She shrugged. 'Some time in March, I think.'

'I'll take holidays,' her mother vowed. 'I want to be there for you.' There was a slight pause. 'And the daddy?'

'He doesn't know yet...and he's not going to be thrilled. I...um...got him all wrong.'

'Oh, darling.'

Kit's eyes filled at the sympathy in her mother's voice. 'Do you really think I have to tell him?' Keeping it from him, would that be so bad?

'Yes, darling, you must.'

Kit knew her mother was right.

'Are you quite sure you got him so wrong?'

'Quote: I don't do long-term. I don't do happy families.

End quote. I don't think he could've made it any plainer, do you?'

Her mother exhaled one indignant breath.

She shook her head at the remembered pain of his words. It didn't matter. Not any more. 'It was a learning experience. The baby and I will be just fine. We'll be better off without him.'

'I'm sure you will be,' her mother agreed, 'but what about him? Will he be better off without you and the baby?'

She snorted. 'Of course not. But, as you and Grandma have always said, you can lead a horse to water…' Still, if Alex did want to be involved…

'I see.' A pause. 'Not all men are like your father, Kitty-Kat.'

She smiled at the childhood nickname. 'I know, Mum. And I will tell him about the baby. Just as soon as he gets back from Africa next month.' And who knew, maybe Alex would surprise her.

'Good. So tell me…'

She had a vision of her mother settling into her favourite armchair, feet tucked beneath her.

'What are your plans? Do you mean to stay in Sydney?'

What was she going to do? Kit wriggled around until she lay on her back. She propped an ankle on the arm of the sofa. She'd never envisaged raising children in the city. She'd always thought…

She gave a sudden laugh as she realized exactly what she was going to do. 'I'm going to go home, Mum. I'm going to raise my child in Tuncurry. It was a wonderful place to grow up.'

'Your grandmother will be thrilled!'

Kit started mentally writing her resignation letter. She'd give two weeks' notice on Monday.

CHAPTER TWO

'GOOD morning, Mr Hallam.'

'Phillip.' Alex inclined his head as he exited the elevator on the top floor of Hallam Enterprises' Sydney office. He told himself that eventually he'd get used to seeing Phillip rather than Kit behind that desk.

'It's good to have you back, sir.'

'Thank you.' Alex walked through to his office. He closed the door behind him and glanced around. Everything was neat, tidy and shining. Outside the window, the harbour sparkled in the early spring sunlight.

Nothing had changed.

Except Kit no longer sat at that desk in the foyer.

It had been almost four months since he and Kit had...

He dragged a hand down his face to try and dispel images that were still far too vivid.

He dropped into his chair. This last month in Africa had provided him with some perspective, given him some distance. It had renewed his determination, had allowed him to gather his strength again. With Kit, he'd made a mistake. He'd paid dearly for that mistake too. He'd made love to her and in the next instant the nightmares about little Chad had started up again. He couldn't go there, couldn't do that again. Not for anyone. Not even for Kit.

He'd learned his lesson and he would never make the same mistake again. Not with Kit. Not with any woman.

He swung in his chair to survey the harbour, a scowl building through him. Reckless. Idiotic. That was what he'd been. He should've taken more care around her. He should've...

He shouldn't have hurt her.

The knowledge that he had pounded at him, lashed him with guilt. Even now. She deserved so much more than anything he could ever offer her. She deserved the best. She would never find the best with him. He didn't do family, forever and commitment. He couldn't do it.

He tried to focus on the scene before him, willed himself to appreciate its beauty. When that didn't work he dragged a hand down his face. It took an effort of will to stop his shoulders from slumping. He'd regret hurting Kit till the day he died, that was something he couldn't change. But no doubt she'd found a way to move on and so had he.

There was just one more test.

He leant across and pressed a button on his intercom. 'Phillip, can you set up a meeting with Kit Mercer for some time tomorrow afternoon.'

There was a hesitation at the other end of the line. 'Sir, Kit resigned. All the details are in a file in your in-box. She finished up at the end of the week before last.'

Alex didn't say anything. He sat back and stared at the intercom. He stared at his in-box. He tried to work out how he felt.

Betrayal. And relief.

The betrayal was nonsense. Kit owed him nothing.

He rubbed the back of his neck. Relief? Maybe she was right. Maybe this was the answer—cut all ties and never clap eyes on each other again.

He leapt up, paced, stopped to track the Manly ferry's

progress into Circular Quay, and remembered Kit telling him how much she loved working for Hallam Enterprises. She'd said it was her dream job. He remembered her smile, the way her eyes had shone…and her gratitude to him. *To him!* His mouth dried. That had been the same day they'd clinched the Dawson deal, and that night they'd made love.

His hands clenched. He recalled how, in their few meetings since then, two faint lines would appear on her forehead whenever she looked at him and how her eyes would dim. He'd taken her dream job, all the satisfaction she found in her work, and had turned it to ashes.

Letting her walk away, never having to see her again, that would be easy. It'd also be incredibly selfish. Kit had loved her job. She shouldn't be made to suffer on his account any more than she already had. He had to make this right!

He swore loud and hard. That was what his trip to Africa had been about—wanting to do something positive rather than negative, helping rather than hurting, making someone's life a bit better rather than a bit worse. He'd needed to feel that he could make a difference in a good way instead of a bad one.

Letting Kit walk away was making a difference in a bad way. He'd done enough damage where she was concerned. He had no intention of adding to the score.

He scattered the contents of his in-box across his desk until he found the file he wanted. He tucked it under his arm. 'Tell Donald he's still in charge,' he shot at Phillip as he strode from his office. He punched the button for the elevator…twice…three times. 'There's something I need to take care of.'

Phillip did his best not to gape. Kit would've stood, hands on hips, and demanded to know where he was going, what time he'd be back and what he expected her to tell all his appointments for the day. Alex shot into the elevator before Phillip could ask him anything so unanswerable.

All of those answers depended on Kit.

Alex double-checked the file that lay open on the car seat beside him, and glanced again at the house opposite. There was no doubt about it, this was the address. This was where Kit now lived.

He frowned. It was a far cry from her stylish one-bedroom flat in French's Forest. That building had been all square blonde brick with a couple of well-trimmed hibiscuses out the front. This wasn't anywhere near as well-ordered. This was…messy.

Paint peeled from weatherboards, and one end of the tiny veranda sagged. What lawn there was needed cutting. Shrubs grew willy-nilly in the front garden. Most of it was obscured, though, by the enormous bottlebrush tree on the front path that was so laden with red blossoms it sagged beneath their weight. It took him a moment to realize the hum came from the bees in that tree rather than his shock.

Kit's talents would be wasted in this two-horse town.

He'd researched Tuncurry on his phone at a roadside restaurant a couple of hours back. Apparently it was a sea-side township purportedly inundated with holidaymakers in the summer, four hours north of Sydney. A glance at his watch told him he'd been on the road for five hours.

Five hours? He hadn't even had the sense to pack an overnight bag. He dragged both hands back through his hair. He didn't even have a plan.

He did know the outcome he wanted, though. For Kit to return to Hallam Enterprises.

He pushed out of the car and straightened his tie. All he had to do was the right thing. He had to make things right for Kit again so she could go back to the job she loved. End of story.

The gate squeaked when he opened it and the wood and wire fence swayed when the gate slammed back into place behind him. The door to the house stood wide open, but nobody appeared at his first knock, or his second.

He hesitated, then opened the screen door. 'Hello?'

The room was empty—unlived in empty. No furniture. No people. He was about to holler another hello when a door at what he guessed was the back of the house thudded closed and a few seconds later Kit came tripping into the room wearing faded jeans, a navy-blue singlet top and with her hair scraped back into a ponytail. He cleared his throat. She swung to him and froze in one of the shafts of sunlight that came streaming in through the front windows.

His stomach hollowed out. Dear Lord, she was lovely. A sense of regret stole through him, giving him the strength to push his shoulders back. 'Hello, Kit.' He took two steps into the room and let the screen door close behind him.

'Alex?'

Two lines creased her forehead. He had an insane urge to walk across and smooth them out.

'What on earth are you doing here? I thought you'd ring or email, but…'

The sound of a truck screeching to a halt outside had her glancing behind him. 'You'll have to excuse me for a minute.' She shook herself, dusted off her hands. 'It sounds as if my new furniture has arrived.'

She moved past him and out to the veranda to wave to the truck. She smelled of soap and fresh cotton and she barely spared him a glance. He surveyed the room in an effort to distract himself from the way her jeans hugged the curve of her hips, at the memory of how his hands had traced those curves and how she'd—

His heart started to pound. He gritted his teeth. He glanced to his left, guessing the hallway that opened off there led to the bedrooms and bathroom. Given the proportions of the outside of the house, he'd guess there would be two bedrooms.

The mundane calculations helped settle his heart rate.

Kit half-turned in the doorway, not quite meeting his eyes, and smiled as if he could be anyone. 'How was Africa?'

'Amazing.' He found himself suddenly eager to tell her all about it. He knew she'd appreciate it, that she'd understand. He opened his mouth to find she'd already swung away to greet a burly man with a clipboard.

'Delivery for Mercer?'

'That'd be me,' Kit said with a smile that held genuine warmth, and Alex's stomach dropped. Kit didn't want to hear about his trip. And there was no conceivable reason on earth why she should be glad to see him.

'Do you need a hand?'

The burly man glanced at Alex, took in the suit and tie and shook his head. 'We'll be right, mate. We do this for a living.' He turned back to Kit. 'Just tell us where you'd like the stuff.'

Bemused, Alex watched as Kit indicated where she wanted the dining table and chairs—in the small part of the L-shaped living room, which he discovered adjoined the kitchen with a door that led out to the back garden.

'I want the dresser there, the sofas here and here, and the entertainment unit against that wall.'

'Rightio. Oh, and the boss was really sorry the delivery was delayed so he sent someone to install those shelves you ordered.'

'That was kind of him. I want them on that wall there.'

She indicated an internal wall and Alex had never felt more like a third wheel in his life.

She turned to look at him again. And again those two lines creased her forehead. 'We'll um…be out the back if you need us.'

'No probs.'

Kit hitched her head in the direction of the back garden and Alex followed. Her back garden wasn't any neater than the front. A row of haphazard azaleas bloomed along the fence to the right. A banksia stood sentinel at the back fence while, to the right, a giant frangipani stood wedged between the back of the house and a garden shed, threatening to push them both over. Some patches of the lawn were more sand than grass.

Kit, however, didn't seem to find anything wrong with the place and she certainly wouldn't care what his opinion of it was either. That much was evident.

'Are you just passing through, Alex, or is there a purpose to your visit?'

Her ponytail bounced as she knelt down in front of a Cape Cod chair, picked up a piece of coarse sandpaper and started sanding.

His stomach started to cramp. He felt ridiculous in his dark suit and tie out here in her garden. He dragged the tie from around his neck and shoved it into his jacket pocket. He undid his top button and ordered himself to take a deep breath. 'There's a reason.'

Her ponytail kept bobbing. She was sanding that chair all wrong. If she weren't careful, she'd pull a muscle. He had to clench his hands to stop from reaching out, hauling her to her feet and turning her to face him.

He couldn't touch her. He'd made so much progress and he had no intention of backsliding now. He just wanted to make things right—do the right thing. Touching her would be a step in the wrong direction.

'Then any time today would be good…'

His teeth clenched when she still didn't turn around. He unclenched them to say, 'I'm waiting for you to spare me a moment of your attention.'

'From memory, when you were offered my full attention you didn't want it.'

Just like that, the old tension wrapped around them. Her hand froze mid-sand as if she couldn't believe she'd uttered the words.

He wanted to swear and swear and swear. He should've had a plan. He should've rehearsed what to say. He should've known better than to trust his instincts when he was anywhere in the vicinity of Kit Mercer.

'You resigned!' The words shot out of him like an accusation. Unrehearsed.

'You always were quick on the uptake.'

Kit had always been sassy, but rarely sarcastic. His hands clenched and this time he did swear. 'Can't we try and keep this civilised?'

Finally she turned and planted herself in the half-sanded chair. 'Why?'

All his frustration bubbled up, threatening to choke him. 'Look, I didn't force you to sleep with me, all right? We were consenting adults and you were as into it as I was. I know I didn't live up to your expectations and I'm sorry. I wish to God it had never happened. But it's done now and I can't undo it.'

Her eyes hardened. 'Fine!'

'What else can I do, other than apologise?'

'Leave?'

The word kicked him in the centre of his gut and he knew then that this woman had left her mark on him for life. He also knew that if he was to save his sanity he had to rip her out of his life completely.

But he should be the one to suffer. Not her.

'I can't accept your resignation, Kit.'

An angry flush stained her cheeks. Her eyes glittered. 'That's your problem, Alex, not mine.'

'You loved your job!'

'So?'

'And you were brilliant at it.'

She blinked.

'Come back to Hallam Enterprises and I will double your salary.'

'No.'

'I'll triple it.' He planted his feet. 'Kit, you're too valuable an employee to give up on without a fight.'

She stared up at him and he could've sworn her bottom lip wobbled. 'Alex—'

'Look, come back. You don't need to relocate and change your whole way of life. If working with me is so difficult for you, I'll relocate instead to our Brisbane office. I will leave Donald in charge of operations in Sydney, I'll triple your salary and you won't have to clap eyes on me again. I promise.'

Her eyes had grown huge. She pressed her hands to her cheeks. 'I thought you'd ring, Alex, or email. I didn't expect you to just turn up like this.'

Her hands shook. Her colour kept flooding and then receding. Should he have given her some warning? He'd been so intent on his mission he hadn't thought what might be best for her.

But he knew how much she'd loved her job. She gained more satisfaction out of her job as project manager than he did running the entire company. She shouldn't feel compelled to leave because of what had happened between them.

Still, he'd been a fool to think that any meeting between them could be anything less than fraught.

He raked both hands back through his hair. In the warm spring sunshine his skin started to prickle beneath his suit jacket. 'Why don't I come back tomorrow at, say, 10:00 a.m.? It'll give you a chance to think over my offer. You're obviously busy here and—'

'No!' She surged to her feet. 'I don't want to drag this out. Alex, I will not be returning to Sydney. I mean to make this place home. I grew up in Tuncurry and I've missed it. This is where I want to live. The lifestyle, the people, the pace, it suits me more than Sydney ever did.'

Didn't she care that her talents would be wasted here?

'Your offer was more than generous—' she hauled in a breath '—and I do appreciate it, but…'

She didn't finish her sentence. She didn't have to. Her shrug said it all. Bile rose up to burn his throat, his tongue. His recklessness, his *weakness*, had made this woman's life worse and there was nothing he could do to make amends. 'What will you do?'

'I'll get a job. I have a lot of contacts here and the tourism industry is thriving. With my qualifications, it'll be a piece of cake.'

She had every right to that confidence. Whoever was lucky enough to employ her would find they had a gem.

'You're sure you won't reconsider?'

She shook her head. And then she went so pale he found himself stepping forward to take her arm. She lifted her hands to ward him off. Stepped away so he couldn't touch her. As if his touch would poison her. Just for a moment he had to rest his hands on his knees.

'Alex, I don't want to raise my children in the city. I want to raise them here.'

He flinched at that word—*children*—and then straightened, but part of him was glad—fiercely glad—that she'd uttered it. It reminded him of the impossible gulf that lay between them.

Her lips twisted and her eyes hardened at whatever she saw reflected in his face. But her colour didn't return. He noted the way she twisted her hands together. To stop them from shaking?

'Alex, I didn't resign from Hallam Enterprises because I found it impossible to work with you. I resigned because I'm pregnant.'

He stared. For a moment it seemed as if time were suspended. And then her last two words hit him in the stomach like blows from a sledgehammer. *I'm pregnant.*

I'm pregnant. I'm pregnant.

No! He fell back. Not... *No!* 'You can't be serious?' The words rasped from a throat that burned like acid.

'I've never been more serious about anything in my life.'

Her hands twisted and twisted. He stared at them and prayed they could save him. 'With...?'

But he couldn't finish the question. He reeled away from her, reeled all the way to the back fence and the banksia tree. He dug his fingers into the hard bark of a branch and held on until the nausea passed. Anger pounded through him then, hot and thick and suffocating. At the edge of his consciousness he could hear Chad's laughter taunting him like it did in his nightmares.

He swung around, strode back to where Kit stood and jabbed a finger at her. 'You expect me to believe it's mine?' The words were harsher than anything that had ever scraped out of his throat before.

She folded her arms, moistened her lips and met his glare head on, although tears filled her eyes and he doubted she could see him properly through them. But she didn't let a single one of them fall. 'Just walk away, Alex,' she whispered. 'Just turn around and walk away and we'll pretend that none of this ever happened.'

His heart pounded in his throat, his pulse raced. He'd come here to make her the offer of a lifetime. Instead, she was extending that offer to him.

He could walk away.

He didn't want to walk. He wanted to run!

CHAPTER THREE

ALEX lurched across to the nearest azalea bush, where he promptly and comprehensively vomited. Kit had to sit again and focus on her breathing to avoid that urge herself. Up to this point, her pregnancy had been remarkably nausea free.

She rubbed at the niggling ache in her back. In her free moments, when she'd tried to picture telling Alex he was going to be a father, she'd expected yelling and shouting, accusations and disbelief, even a hard, angry silence.

Shock—yes.

Vomiting—no.

Had her father vomited when her mother had told him she was pregnant with Kit?

She shook the thought off and deepened the massage to the left side of her back, her fingers doing what they could to shift the pain there and their own nervousness. With Alex, she'd have preferred the shouting and anger. A part of her would have preferred it if he'd taken the out she'd offered him and had walked away without one single backward glance. She flicked a quick glance in his direction.

He still might yet.

She tried to stamp out the sympathy that rose through her at the memory of the white-lipped panic that had sent him wheeling away from her, at the red-faced panic that had sent him hurtling back, at the grey-skinned despair that had sent him staggering across to that azalea bush.

Having an unplanned baby wasn't the end of the world!

Her throat ached. Her eyes stung. Her news had made him vomit. *Vomit!*

I don't do happy families.

He wasn't kidding, was he?

Her temples throbbed. The ache in her back that had been plaguing her since yesterday increased in ferocity. A hot flush wrung her out and then a chill gripped her. She might not be able to stop herself from feeling sorry for Alex, but he was an adult, a grown up. He might not do happy families, but she did. There was no way on God's green that she was going to let him hurt her baby.

Their baby.

No—her baby! Alex didn't want this child. She did with every molecule of her being. She would provide for this baby and give it everything it needed.

A baby needs a father.

She thrust her chin out. She'd coped perfectly well without one.

Really?

She dropped her head to her hands with a groan. She'd ached to have a father who'd wanted her, who'd loved her.

'Kit?'

Alex's face was void of all emotion. It made her catch her breath. How could he hide all that…that *turmoil* away, just like that? She searched his face for a spark of…anything.

She searched in vain.

'You're saying it's mine?'

'Yes.'

'We used protection.'

She didn't want to do this. She wanted to curl up and sleep the afternoon away. She wanted to forget all about Alex Hallam. 'We'd have been better off if I'd been on the Pill.'

'Have you thought everything through? Considered all your options?' He planted his hands on his hips, his eyes narrowed. 'You know you have options, don't you?'

'You're talking about a termination?'

'That's certainly one of your options and—'

That had her surging to her feet. She ignored the pain that cramped her back. 'What a typically male thing to say! You're…' She couldn't find words enough to describe the entirety of his awfulness.

He wanted her to get rid of their beautiful baby?

Oh, that so wasn't going to happen!

'Look, I'm just saying it's an option, that's all. I was just checking that you'd considered *all* your options.'

'Is that so?' She folded her arms. After the heat of her first flush of anger she went cold all over. Chilled-to-the-bone cold. 'But a termination would make your life so much easier, wouldn't it?'

'Only if the child is mine.'

For a moment she couldn't breathe. He doubted it? He thought she would lie about something as important as this? She'd envisaged anger and shock, resentment, when she told Alex the news but not once had it occurred to her that he might not believe her. She'd never given him any reason to think she would lie.

She wrapped her arms about her middle to stop from falling apart. 'I am not terminating my pregnancy.'

He didn't blink. He didn't flinch. 'Fine. But if you claim the child is mine then I demand a paternity test be carried out upon the child's birth.'

She hitched up her chin. 'Alex, you've made it clear

from the start that you're not a family man.' Well, perhaps not exactly from the start. But he had rectified that particular misapprehension on her part with startling speed. 'I don't want anything from you. I assure you I have everything that I need. Frankly, I don't know what you are still doing here.'

His gaze sliced to the path that led around the side of the house—the path that would take him to his car and freedom. She recognized the hunger that flashed across his face before all expression was cut off again.

'I—'

An almighty crash from within the house interrupted whatever he'd been about to say. Kit spun around. One of the deliverymen appeared at the back door. 'I…uh…a wall's fallen down.'

She blinked. 'It's what?' She took off at a run. Her beautiful house!

'Kit, wait, it might not be safe!'

She ignored Alex's shout. It couldn't be any more dangerous than being out in the back garden with him. His footsteps pounded behind her, but he didn't catch up with her until she came to a dead halt at the edge of the living room. He slammed into her and she winced as pain cramped her back again. She coughed at the plaster dust thick in the air.

'Sorry.' He gripped her shoulders to steady her. 'Okay?'

She couldn't answer him. The warmth of his hands had memories sideswiping her, memories that demanded she turn and rest herself in his arms. Crazy! She couldn't talk but she could resist such insane impulses. She managed a nod.

He immediately transferred his attention to the deliverymen. 'Anyone hurt?'

She closed her eyes. She was a hundred different kinds of a fool where this man was concerned.

The deliverymen all assured Alex that they were unhurt and Kit opened her eyes to survey the damage. She waved a hand in front of her face to try and dispel some of the dust. 'What happened?'

Her house. Her beautiful house.

As the dust settled, a great hole appeared in her wall where her brand new shelves should've been. They lay in disarray amidst the clutter and mess on the floor. Alex swore. 'Didn't you look for a supporting beam?'

'Course I did,' a dusty figure muttered. 'Take a look yourself.'

Alex did. He poked and prodded and then swore at whatever he'd discovered. Kit's heart sank. Her budget didn't run to expensive repairs and—

All her thoughts slammed to a halt when he stuck his head through the hole and peered upwards. 'Alex!' The protest squeaked out of her. What if more stuff fell down?

It was only when he backed out again that she noticed the three deliverymen edging towards the door. 'What do you think you're doing?' She'd meant to utter the words in her best scary secretary voice, but it came out as a squeak too.

'Sorry, love, but we've delivered your furniture. There's nothing more we can do here.' With that they turned tail and fled.

'Hold on a minute!'

A firm hand wrapping around her upper arm prevented her from setting off after them. 'It's not their fault, Kit. Let them go.'

She wrenched herself out of his grip and then coughed as dust rose up around them, disturbed by her agitated movements. It settled on the shoulders, the sleeves, the lapels of Alex's finely tailored suit. It settled everywhere, even on his eyelashes. Kit yanked her gaze away. She didn't want to notice how the dust on his eyelashes made the brown of his irises deeper and clearer. She didn't want to notice anything about Alex Hallam.

He went to take her arm, but she evaded him. She didn't want him touching her again either. She didn't want to notice how his touch was imprinted on her soul. As if she were his woman. She wasn't!

She whirled away from him. 'What do you know about any of this anyway?'

He brushed a hand through his hair, shaking plaster dust out of it. He shrugged and sort of grimaced. 'I'm a builder by trade, Kit.'

'No, you're not. You're a multi-millionaire property developer.' She planted her feet. 'Builder my foot,' she muttered under her breath.

'I'm a multi-millionaire property developer *and* a builder by trade.'

She frowned. 'But you have an economics degree.' She'd seen it on the wall of his office.

'Mature-age entry. Part-time attendance. How do you think I funded a tertiary education?'

She stared at him and then shook her head. Had she ever really known him?

All the intimate ways she had known him rose up through her. When he raised an eyebrow she realized she was staring. She pushed the memories away and bit her lip, wished it weren't so hard to catch her breath. 'So…' she waved at the hole in the wall '…you know about all this?'

He nodded.

She bit back a sigh. 'Right then, you'd better tell me the worst.'

He glanced at the wall and then back at her. A frown formed in his eyes. 'The wall stud is rotten with damp. That's why it didn't hold the shelves and, as you can see, when they fell they took a great chunk of plaster with them. Kit, there's a hole in the roof. Looks as if you'll need to find a new place to rent.'

'I'm not renting, Alex.' Kit wanted to sink to the floor amid all the chaos and rest for a bit. 'I've bought this house. It belongs to me.'

Alex pushed his jacket back to plant his hands on his hips. 'How the hell does one buy a house in just three weeks?'

'Private sale.' Her hands rested in the small of her back as she grimaced and stretched. 'We rushed it through.'

The owners had seen her coming a mile off. 'At least tell me you had a building inspection done.'

'The previous owners told me it was fine. The real estate agent said he could vouch for them personally.'

'Did you get anything in writing?'

He knew the answer before she shook her head. How could a woman so savvy and efficient in dealing with demanding clients and difficult staff make such an elementary mistake? His gaze drifted to her waist and his lips thinned.

She rested her hands on her knees and only then did he notice how unwell she looked. Pregnant women, they threw up a lot, right? He grimaced at the reminder of his own behaviour earlier. 'Kit, are you going to be sick?'

'Don't think so,' she mumbled.

She straightened. He noticed the way her hand went to the small of her back as if trying to massage away a pain there. He did a rough calculation. If he were the father, Kit would be nearly four months into her pregnancy. He couldn't remember when Jacqueline had started getting back pain. He was pretty sure it was later than four months. 'Are you sure you're feeling all right?'

'I'm pregnant,' she snapped. 'I don't have some disease!'

He figured he deserved that, but…he really didn't like her colour.

'And it's been a great day,' she continued. 'The father of my child throws up when I tell him the happy news and now I have a hole not only in my wall but, if what you are telling me is true, in my roof too! You know what, Alex? I'm feeling on top of the world right now.'

She had a point. Several, in fact. Rather valid points at that. He couldn't help it. He glanced at her waist again. As far as he could tell, there wasn't any change there at all.

Perhaps this could turn out to be a glorious mistake?

He glanced at the hole in the wall and knew he was grasping at straws. Kit had a hole in her wall *and* she was pregnant.

He was in the middle of a nightmare.

He was going to suffocate. All the plaster dust in the room felt as if it had lodged in his throat. He didn't do kids. He didn't do family. *He wanted out of here.*

He dragged in a hoarse gasp of air and closed his eyes, concentrating on his breathing. Kit had told him he could walk away.

He wanted to run, escape, as fast as he could.

He wanted to stampede for the door. Charge through it and never come back.

He opened his eyes, glanced at the door and then glanced at Kit, who'd backed up to perch on the edge of the nearest sofa, which was still wrapped in the heavy-duty plastic it had arrived in. He frowned as he looked at her more closely. One moment she was pale, the next she was flushed. Before he had time to think better of it, he reached out and rested the back of his hand against her forehead.

She slapped it away. Glared. 'What do you think you're doing?'

She was burning up!

He dragged a hand back through his hair. His retreat was moving further and further out of reach. He could almost feel it slipping through his fingers like water…or plaster dust.

'You're running a temperature.' Hell! He couldn't leave a sick woman to fend for herself. 'Come on. You need a doctor to check you over. I'll take you up to the hospital.'

'Don't be ridiculous!'

By rights, her glare should've withered him to the spot. He sat next to her, he was careful not to touch her. 'You're not feeling well, Kit, and you're running a temperature so you can be excused for making poor judgement calls.'

'Poor judge—'

'But do you really want to take the risk that a high temperature might harm your baby?'

'Oh!'

Her bottom lip wobbled and one of her hands moved to cradle her abdomen. That action told him exactly how much this baby meant to her. For a moment he had to fight the nausea that punched through him again.

'You really think I'm running a temperature?'

'I know it.'

'Okay,' she finally whispered. 'But not the hospital, the medical clinic.'

'Fine.' He would take her to see a doctor. He would bring her home again. He'd book into a hotel overnight. Tomorrow, he and Kit would discuss what needed discussing and then he would walk out of her life for ever.

CHAPTER FOUR

Kɪᴛ's pallor, the way she bit her bottom lip and her down-turned mouth all struck at Alex's heart, making him forget his own panic. He wished he could make her smile. He'd been able to—once.

He stood and pretended to survey the sofas. 'You know what? The plastic-wrapped look was a smart choice. I think it could really take off.'

She didn't smile.

'I hear babies make a lot of mess. You might want to keep this look for the next three or four years.'

He couldn't believe he'd said the word *babies* without flinching. 'You know, we could plastic-wrap the whole interior of this room. You could just hose it down at the end of every day. It'd save you loads of time.' He was glad he'd made the effort when her lips shifted upwards the tiniest fraction.

He shook himself. Enough of this. 'C'mon, let's get you to the medical clinic.' He reached down and helped her to her feet. He didn't release her arm. 'Are you feeling dizzy or faint?' Should he carry her to the car?

His skin pulled tight with need. It rocked him to find just how much he wanted to touch her, to have her in his arms.

She shook her head. Carefully, as if the action hurt. 'I

just feel as if I have a bad case of the flu without the sore throat and sniffles.'

His chest clenched. The sooner she saw a doctor the sooner she'd get medicine—antibiotics or whatnot—to make her feel better. But when she removed her arm from his grasp all he could think for a moment was how the day had darkened. They were just about to leave when they found the door blocked by two figures.

'Hello, lovey, we're Frank and Doreen from next door.' An elderly couple tripped into the room. 'Hello, Kit dear.'

He blinked. *Lovey?* Him? Nobody...*nobody* had *ever* called him lovey. He rolled his shoulders, cracked his neck.

'Hi, Auntie Doreen.'

Her aunt!

'The boys just told us what happened. We thought we'd pop our heads in to see if there's anything we can do.' Doreen turned to Alex. 'Frank here used to be a welder, you know.'

Frank here looked about seventy in the shade.

'He's handy with his hands.'

And then she winked at him.

Alex swallowed back a smart rejoinder. How on earth did a welder propose to fix a hole in a wall, not to mention another in the roof? Even if he was *handy with his hands*.

Nevertheless, when the older man extended his hand Alex shook it. 'Alex Hallam.' He glanced at Kit. She looked ready to drop. 'I'm sorry, but Kit is running a temperature. We're off to the medical clinic.' He waved a hand at the mess. 'I'll deal with all this later.'

'You run along, lovey, while we see what we can do.'

He didn't want this unconventional pair messing with Kit's house. Things were bad enough already.

'We'll close the door when we leave.'

Kit didn't seem concerned or put out by Doreen's words so he shrugged and edged her towards the door.

Doreen leant across to squeeze Kit's hand as they passed. 'So glad your young man has finally arrived.'

'Oh, but he isn't—'

'Young,' Alex bit out. He continued to shepherd her all the way out of the door and towards his car. They didn't have time for explanations.

Alex accompanied Kit into the doctor's consulting room. She didn't put up a fight, but he had a feeling that had more to do with how unwell she was feeling rather than a sign of her trust in him.

The doctor frowned and pointed to a chair when Alex started pacing up and down. He planted himself in it and tried not to fidget. Then he scowled. The doctor looked as if he was just out of high school! Surely he was too young to know which way was up, let alone—

'Relax, Alex,' Kit groaned.

Relax? How could he relax when she looked like death warmed up? Why hadn't he picked up on that earlier? He could have unknowingly made her worse. He'd walked into her house as if he'd had every right and demanded she come back to work. Without a thought for what she really wanted. All to ease his conscience. As if he knew what would make her happiest. As if he knew what was best for her.

He knew zilch.

He dragged a hand back through his hair. He did know one thing. When a woman told you she was pregnant with your child, you shouldn't throw up. Bad reaction. Wrong reaction. Completely inappropriate.

And completely out of his control.

But…Kit was carrying *his child*?

He slammed a wall down on that thought.

Not his baby, Kit's. And if Kit lost her baby because of anything he'd done—

Bile rose up to burn his throat. He choked it back. He would never forgive himself if that happened. Never.

'Kit, you have a kidney infection. I suspect you've had a urinary tract infection, not all that unusual during pregnancy, which has travelled to your kidneys.'

Alex's head snapped up at the doctor's words. 'How serious is that?' he barked. It sounded bad.

Kit didn't look at him, but her hands shook. He clenched his to fists. 'What he said,' she whispered.

'We've caught it early.'

Her hands cradled her abdomen and Alex couldn't take his eyes from them. Such small, fragile hands.

'Will my baby be okay?'

'Yes. As long as you do everything I say.'

Kit swallowed and nodded. Alex leaned forward to make sure he caught every word the doctor uttered.

'I'm booking you in for an ultrasound on...' he surveyed his computer '...on Thursday. It'll put both you and your regular doctor's minds at rest. I'll also prescribe you a course of antibiotics, and no, they won't harm your baby,' he added before Kit could ask. 'But, until your ultrasound, I want you to have complete bed rest.'

'Oh, but—'

'You can get up to go to the bathroom. You can have a quick shower or tepid bath once a day. But the rest of the time I want you in bed.'

Kit's hands twisted in her lap. 'I...'

The doctor peered at her over the top of his glasses. 'It's better to be safe than sorry, isn't it?'

'Yes, of course. It's just...'

The doctor turned to Alex. 'She'll need someone to stay with her, look after her.'

Alex nodded, ignoring the way his stomach dropped. 'I'll do that.' Thursday? He could stay till Thursday, or even the weekend. Kit wouldn't be sick if she wasn't pregnant. And she wouldn't be pregnant if it wasn't for him.

Thursday or the weekend? It was the least he could do.

He could see that Kit didn't like the idea. In fact, she probably loathed it. Not that he could blame her.

The doctor pointed at Kit. 'You rest. It's important, you hear?'

Kit nodded and swallowed. 'I hear.'

Alex wanted to hit the doctor for frightening her.

The doctor's glare transferred itself to Alex. 'She's to have no stress, no worry. She's not to be upset in any way.'

Alex's hands clenched as fear punched through him then too. 'Right.' No stress, no worry. He could manage that. For Kit. Till Thursday. Or the weekend.

'I don't need you to stay with me, Alex,' Kit said the moment he pulled his car to a halt out the front of her house and turned off the ignition.

He didn't blame her for not wanting him there. In her shoes he wouldn't want him staying over either, but hadn't she heard a word the doctor said? She needed someone to stay with her, look after her. He wasn't leaving until someone trustworthy was here to fill his shoes.

'I'm happy to call one of your friends or a relative—perhaps your aunt Doreen—to stay with you, but I'm not leaving you alone, Kit. You heard what the doctor said,' he added when she opened her mouth to argue.

She closed it again. She looked pale and wrung out, and he grimaced. 'Look, this is the story, Kit. I'm staying in Tuncurry tonight. Now, whether that's on one of your new sofas or in a hotel room is up to you.'

'But—'

'It's getting a bit late to be driving back to Sydney, especially when I'm still jet-lagged from the Africa trip.'

She rested her head against the back of the seat as if it were too hard to hold it up under her own steam. He wanted to reach out and trace the line of her jaw, the curve of her cheek. He clenched his hand. Just get her into bed where she can rest. No stress, no worry.

He swallowed. 'Kit, how does this sound for a plan? You let me crash on your sofa, just for tonight, and tomorrow we can discuss other arrangements?'

She closed her eyes and then finally she nodded. 'Okay.'

He had a feeling she'd agree to just about anything at the moment if it meant she could rest.

He discovered that didn't mean she'd let him carry her into the house, though. He stayed close behind her on the slow trek from the car to the house, in case she needed a hand. They both paused on the threshold. The living room looked like a bombsite, though Frank and Doreen had obviously done their best to sweep the debris into one tidy pile.

Kit picked up a note from the coffee table. 'Doreen has left us a casserole.' She started to turn. 'I should pop over and thank her.'

'I'll do that. You go to bed.'

She didn't look at him. She glanced about the room and her shoulders slumped. One of her small hands inched across her stomach. Alex's chest burned. She looked so lost and alone. He touched her shoulder, but when she glanced up at him with big worry-filled eyes he found himself drawing her into his arms and pressing her head to the hollow of his shoulder. 'It's going to be okay, Kit.'

'You don't know that,' she mumbled, but she didn't draw away.

He stroked her hair in an effort to reassure her, but found himself revelling in her softness, in how good she smelt, instead. 'We'll do everything the doctor says and you and your baby will be fine.'

She stared up at him then, a frown in her eyes.

'If the doctor had been really worried he'd have admitted you to hospital.'

She nodded, but the frown didn't leave her eyes. 'What are you still doing here, Alex?'

'There are things we need to talk about.' Maybe honesty would win him a measure of her trust. 'It doesn't matter how much I might want to leave, I can't until we've thrashed some things out. But that can wait until later in the week. What's important at the moment is for you to get better again.'

He hooked an arm under her knees and lifted her into his arms. Carrying her was easier than arguing with her.

Carrying her was divine.

'Point me in the direction of your bedroom.'

She pointed to the corridor that led off the living room. 'First door on the right.'

The moment he set foot inside it, he wanted to back out again. This bedroom, with its big wooden bed and plaid quilt in pastel shades piled decadently with cushions, was pure Kit. It reminded him of *that night*.

He set her down on her bed and then backed up fast, almost falling over his feet in his haste. 'You need to rest—doctor's orders. Nothing else matters at the moment, Kit. I'll go and serve you up a plate of your aunt's casserole.' Even sick, she looked divine.

'Honorary aunt. Doreen isn't my real aunt.'

Right.

'Alex?'

He turned in the doorway.

Her chin lifted as she met his gaze. 'You're going to leave us, aren't you, me and our baby?'

Her bottom lip wobbled as the words whispered out of her. Each word pierced his flesh.

She bit her lip, maybe in an attempt to get it back under control, and then she pursed her mouth. 'You know, Alex, I can understand you not wanting a future with me. I get that.'

She glanced away, swallowed. Her throat worked. He wanted to close his eyes.

She turned and her gaze met his again, her eyes dark and shadowed. Confusion and turmoil chased themselves across her face. 'But how can you turn your back on our baby?'

A weight slammed into place. He must look like a monster in her eyes.

Maybe he was.

He wanted to tell her to rest but the words wouldn't come.

'You don't care what's best for me. You don't care what's best for our baby. All you care about is what's best for you.'

She spoke almost as if to herself and her words chilled him. He wanted to tell her she was wrong, but...

He shook himself. 'Kit, I'm not abandoning you. I will be staying until the weekend.'

Her lips twisted. 'What good do you think that will do anyone?'

He didn't know how to answer.

She shifted slightly, her eyes suddenly glittering. 'You know what? It might just be simpler if I make you a lump sum payment.'

'What the hell...?'

'For the donation of your sperm. That way, everyone knows exactly where they stand. There'll be no misunderstandings.' She lifted her chin. 'I'm sure you can get those fancy lawyers of yours to draft something up.'

Horror welled through him. She couldn't be serious! He—

No stress, no worry.

He clenched his hands to fists, drew in a ragged breath and swallowed back the denial that shot through him. Her eyelids had started to grow heavy. A sheen of perspiration filmed her face. She continued to glare at him with her chin hitched up like a warrior's, but he knew a discussion like this couldn't be good for her. 'Rest now, Kit. We'll talk later.'

Not that there was much more to say, he realized, his mouth growing sour with the knowledge. He turned away and headed for the kitchen. Food and making sure Kit rested—he'd focus on what he could do.

An hour later, Alex found himself on Frank and Doreen's front veranda, hand raised to knock on their door. He'd made a deal with Kit—she'd try to sleep and he'd come over and thank Frank and Doreen.

He shifted his feet, scowled at the ground and knocked.

'Lovey!' Doreen appeared. 'C'mon in.'

He shook his head and fought the urge to fidget. 'I don't want to leave Kit for too long in case she needs me. I just—'

'Frank! It's Kit's young man, Alex.'

Alex gritted his teeth.

'Come in and have a beer, young man,' Frank offered.

Again, Alex shook his head. 'The doctor has diagnosed Kit with a kidney infection. She should be fine but he's ordered bed rest for the next few days. I don't want to leave her alone for too long.'

Both Frank and Doreen nodded sagely, as if this made perfect sense. As far as Alex was concerned, the longer he remained in Tuncurry, the less sense anything made.

'Kit wanted me to come over and thank you.' He suddenly realized how grudging that sounded, as if he hadn't appreciated what they'd done—their attempts to tidy up, the casserole. 'I mean we wanted to thank you.' But he and Kit, they weren't a *we* and he didn't want to give the wrong impression. 'Just...' He gave up. 'Thank you. It was thoughtful of you.'

Frank eyed him. 'You're a city boy, right, Alex?' When Alex didn't say anything he added, 'You'll find we're more community-minded out here.'

Community? It took an effort to stop his lips from twisting. From where he was standing, that just meant Kit would probably get stuck with looking after Frank and Doreen in a few years' time when they both started losing their faculties.

Still, they had checked up on her today and that had been a nice thing to do. And they'd made sure she had food.

Both Frank and Doreen looked at him expectantly. He cleared his throat. 'It's nice to know Kit has such good neighbours.'

'No doubt we'll all get better acquainted now you're here, lad.'

Alex took a step back. No way! The expectation, the cosy familiarity, the good-spiritedness, it wrapped around him, threatening to suffocate him, to bury him. He took another step back. 'I...uh...should get back to Kit. Goodnight.'

He turned and fled.

There wasn't any comfort in returning to Kit's house, though. He glared at the hole in her wall and then threw himself down on the nearest sofa. White dust rose up all around him.

His curse ground out from between gritted teeth. He couldn't bolt and leave Kit's living room looking like a demolition site.

If the child she was carrying was his...

He leapt up and stomped off to find a broom, a bucket and some cleaning cloths. Tonight he'd be sleeping on plastic because he wasn't taking the wrapping off the sofas until he'd had a chance to vacuum, and he wasn't vacuuming tonight. It'd wake Kit and she needed to rest.

Alex checked on Kit again at midnight. She'd taken her antibiotics, she'd eaten some dinner and then she'd slept. So far, so good. She needed to get well. He wanted her to get well as soon as possible.

So you can leave?

He tried not to scowl.

From the light of the hallway he caught sight of the title of the book on her bedside table—*What To Expect When You're Expecting*. He picked it up and tiptoed back out into the living room. Lowering himself to the sofa that would be his bed for the night, he turned to the page she had bookmarked.

And froze.

Everything went blank.

The bookmark—it was an ultrasound photograph of Kit's child.

Of his child.

He snapped the book shut and rested his head in his hands. A baby. A child.

He lifted his head, darkness surging up to fill the empty places inside him. He wasn't doing that again. He couldn't.

You don't care what's best for our baby. All you care about is what's best for you.

Kit didn't understand. Him getting out of her and the baby's lives—that would be best for her and the baby.

And for you too.

He nodded heavily. And for him too. It didn't stop a part of him from feeling as if it were dying, though.

When he finally fell asleep that night, Alex had a nightmare about Chad. He raced through a darkened mansion, his legs wooden and heavy, his heart pounding faster and faster as he searched for the two-year-old. Chad's laughter, always just out of reach, taunted him and spurred him on. The rooms in the mansion went on and on. He tried calling out Chad's name but his voice wouldn't work. His legs grew heavier and heavier. It took all his energy to push forward. He pulled open the final door, surged through it, to find himself plummeting off the edge of a cliff.

He woke before he slammed into the jagged rocks at the bottom, breathing hard and with Chad's name on his lips. He lay in the dark and tried to catch his breath, his skin damp and clammy with perspiration. He tried telling himself Chad was safe, living somewhere in Buenos Aires with his mother, but that didn't ease the darkness that stole through his soul.

Before he and Kit had made love, he hadn't had a nightmare about Chad in over ten months.

He shoved the thought away. It wasn't Kit's fault she made him feel things he hadn't felt in a long time. It was his fault for giving in to temptation. Biting back a groan, he pushed up into a sitting position. Past experience told him he would get no more sleep tonight. He dragged a hand down his face. That was okay. There was still plenty of cleaning to do.

A sharp rap on the front door just after nine o'clock had Alex falling over his feet to answer it before the noise of another knock could wake Kit.

The woman who stood on the other side raked him up and down with bold, unimpressed eyes. 'I'm Caro,' she said without preamble. 'Kit's best friend.' She didn't stick her hand out. 'Doreen rang me. I take it you're Alex?'

'That's right.'

She folded her arms. 'I've heard all about you.'

He gathered none of it had been complimentary.

'How's Kit?'

'Asleep,' he ground out.

'All night?'

'She was up—'

She brushed past him into the living room. 'She's not supposed to be up!'

He clenched his jaw till he thought his teeth might snap. He unclenched it to say, 'The doctor said she was allowed up to have a quick shower once a day.' He felt like a schoolboy hauled up in front of the principal. 'She had breakfast, took her antibiotics and now she's sleeping again.'

'You'd better tell me you prepared her breakfast.'

Who the hell did this woman think she was? He was tempted to shove her back out of the door again. 'Look, I'm worried about her too. I mean to make sure she follows the doctor's orders to the letter.'

'I'm going to pop my head in to check on her.'

'Don't wake her,' he growled.

She tossed him a withering glance before disappearing down the hallway that led to Kit's bedroom.

He scowled after her. She had another thing coming if she thought he was offering her coffee.

Darn it! She was Kit's friend. He stalked into the kitchen and put the jug on to boil.

Caro entered moments later. 'You and me—' she pointed to him '—outside, now.'

He blinked. 'Are you calling me out for a fight? I've got to warn you, Caro, I don't hit women.'

She smiled sweetly. 'It should be a walkover then, shouldn't it?' She glared and held the back door open. 'I want to talk to you and I don't want to disturb Kit while I'm doing it.'

And she was itching to bawl him out. It didn't take a degree in economics and a finely honed ability to read people to figure that one out. He decided it might be safer if Caro didn't have a hot drink in her hand. He preceded her out of the door and into the back garden. Kit's bedroom faced the street. They shouldn't disturb her out here.

'How long before you shoot through again?'

Again? What did she mean, again?

He rolled his shoulders and scowled. If he'd known Kit was pregnant he wouldn't have left for Africa when he had. He'd have...*delayed it for a week?* a sarcastic voice muttered in his head.

He thrust out his jaw, folded his arms. 'I'm not leaving today. I told Kit I'd be here for her and I will be. There are things we need to sort out.'

Caro folded her arms too. 'You can forget it if you mean to offer her money.'

'This is none of your damn business.'

'Kit is my best friend. I love her. Can you say the same?'

For a moment he couldn't utter a single word. The same suffocating shroud that had blanketed him at Frank and Doreen's last night twisted about him now.

'Exactly what I thought,' she snorted. 'You're going to turn tail and run.'

'I am not!' he shot back, stung by the loathing in her voice. He'd wanted to bolt yesterday, but he was still here now, wasn't he? 'And I have to pay child support. It's a legal requirement.' That was only honourable and right.

She stuck out a hip. 'You're a right piece of work, aren't you?'

His jaw dropped.

The next moment Caro's face was wreathed in smiles. 'Hey, honey-bun, you're supposed to be in bed.'

He turned to find Kit in the doorway. She raised an eyebrow in his direction. 'You're still here.'

Had she thought he'd do a runner while she was asleep? He straightened. That was exactly what she'd thought. He forced himself to grin—no stress, the doctor had said. 'Sure I'm still here.' She was still convinced he meant to abandon her.

Isn't that exactly what you mean to do?

He bit back an expletive. He wasn't doing happy families, but he thought about that hole in her wall. Someone had to fix it. He could fix it.

He could make sure Kit had everything she needed and that she was ready for the baby before he sailed off into the sunset.

Kit glanced from Caro to him. He did all he could to keep his expression bland. He tried not to groan when she moistened her lips.

'What's going on out here?'

'Caro and I were just having a chat.' He would not upset her. 'You know the doctor's orders. You want me to carry you back to bed?'

'I'm going, I'm going. May I have a chamomile tea?'

'Coming right up.'

Kit disappeared. Caro grabbed his arm before he reached the back door. 'You mess with my friend and I'll come after you with a meat cleaver.'

He held the door open for her, bowed her inside. 'Chamomile tea for you too?'

'Ooh, lovely.'

She'd pay for that smile. He'd sweeten her tea to within an inch of its life.

But one thing had become increasingly clear—he'd come after himself with a meat cleaver if he hurt Kit any more than he already had.

CHAPTER FIVE

'WERE you giving Alex a hard time?' Kit asked after Alex had delivered their teas and then beat a hasty retreat.

'You bet.' Caro grinned. 'I read him the riot act.'

'Oh, Caro!' But Kit couldn't help laughing as her friend kicked off her shoes and climbed up onto the bed beside her.

Caro grimaced when she took a sip of her tea.

'I thought you liked chamomile.'

'I do.' Caro's lips twitched. 'It's just that first sip, you know? Anyway, tell me how you are feeling.'

'Much, much better. My temperature is back to normal and the awful cramps in my back have become a low level ache...much easier to deal with. And I don't feel as if I've been hit by a bus any more either.' She shuddered. 'I thought I was going to be stuck with that back pain for the next six months.'

'Your colour is good. The antibiotics must've kicked in.'

'I think the doctor is being a panic merchant,' Kit grumbled. She almost felt whole again. 'What am I going to do in bed for another two and a half days?'

'It's better to be safe than sorry.'

Which was what Alex had said when he'd brought her breakfast.

Caro took another sip of her tea. 'You don't think he deserved the riot act?'

'I don't know. I…I can't believe he's still here.' Though he had been sort of sweet last night—reassuring and kind. Somehow he'd managed to defuse her misgivings and her awkwardness, without her even realizing it. She wasn't quite sure how. 'He even vacuumed the living room while I was having breakfast if you can believe it.'

And he hadn't thrown up again. Her lips twisted. At least, not that she knew about.

She glanced at her friend and a different emotion surged through her. She took her and Caro's mugs and set them on the bedside table, and then she took Caro's hand. 'I have something really important to ask you.'

'Shoot.'

'Me getting sick like this, it's made me realize a couple of things. I…' Her stomach knotted and a lump lodged in her throat. Caro squeezed her hands but didn't rush her and Kit loved her all the more for it. 'Caro, if something should ever happen to me… I mean, it probably never will…' She hoped to heaven it never did. 'But…but if I died, would you look after my baby? I don't know who else I trust as much as you. Mum and Grandma would help out, of course, and—'

'Yes.'

Caro didn't hesitate. Kit closed her eyes in relief. 'Thank you.' But a weight pressed down on her. If she'd done this right, her baby would have two parents to rely on rather than one. She'd robbed her child of that and she knew, no matter how much she tried, she would never be able to make that up to her baby. Ever.

Unless Alex had changed his mind and wasn't going to walk away from his child after all. It seemed a slim hope.

A tap on her door brought her crashing back. Alex

stood in the doorway. Her chest clenched. Had he heard what she'd just asked Caro? The pinched white lines around his mouth told her he probably had. She swallowed. But he didn't care, did he? Not about her and not about the baby.

He'd wanted her to terminate her pregnancy!

Her heart burned. Sorrow and anger pulsed through her in equal measure. What did he care what safeguards she put in place to take care of *her* baby? He meant to leave again just as soon as it was humanly possible. She was sure of it. Her best guess was that he'd organise for Doreen and Caro to take it in shifts to look after her for the next couple of days so he could hightail it back to Sydney.

Perhaps she should confront him about that right now? It was just that the doctor had ordered her to rest—no stress, no worry. Yesterday she'd been feeling too fuzzy to take those orders in properly. But today… She swallowed. Today she'd do anything to keep her baby healthy. Fighting with Alex, confronting him about his intentions, had to wait. She raised an eyebrow. 'You wanted something?'

He rubbed his nape. He didn't meet her eyes. 'I wanted to check if Caro was staying for a while. I need to pop out to grab a few things.' His voice was devoid of all emotion.

'Pop away,' Caro said with an airy wave of her hand, not even looking at him.

Alex left without saying another word. Kit pleated the quilt cover with her fingers. 'Do you think he'll be back?' Maybe he'd make that dash for Sydney right now.

'Oh, I'm sure of it.'

She didn't understand Caro's grin but, before she could ask for an explanation, her friend said, 'Snooze or a game of gin rummy?'

'Ooh, go on. Break out the cards.'

* * *

The first thing Kit saw when she woke was the framed photograph of her ultrasound picture on her bedside table. She stared at it for a moment before hauling herself into a sitting position and reaching out to pick it up.

'I thought it might help.'

The second thing she saw was Alex sitting in a dining room chair at the bottom of her bed. Her stomach tightened. She dismissed that as a symptom of her kidney infection. 'Help?'

'I thought it might give you added incentive to follow doctor's orders and stay in bed.'

She had no intention of disobeying the doctor's orders—her baby's welfare was too important for that—but Alex's thoughtfulness touched her all the same. She stared down at the picture, lightly ran her fingers over the glass, following the contours that made up her baby.

'I couldn't make head nor tail of it,' he confessed.

It suddenly seemed wildly important to Kit that he did. 'Head here—' she pointed '—tail there.'

Alex didn't move to get a better look and she remembered then that he didn't want this child. She pressed the photo frame to her chest. She wanted to tell her baby that it didn't matter.

Only it did matter. A lot.

'Why are you sitting guard at the end of my bed?'

'I didn't want you getting up again unless you had to. I'm here to fetch and carry.'

Oh.

'Caro said to ring if you needed anything.'

Caro had gone? How long had Kit been asleep for? She and Caro had played cards for over an hour and then she'd napped. She glanced at the clock. She'd napped for three hours! Caro would've had to leave to collect Davey from pre-school.

'Your friend is a psychopath, by the way. Can I get you something to eat or drink?'

Kit's lips twitched. She settled back more comfortably against her pillows. 'No, thank you.' She still had an almost full bottle of water on the bedside table. 'I know Caro can come across as kind of scary, but she has my best interests at heart.'

'I know,' he said softly. 'I'm glad you have such a good friend.'

She was so surprised she couldn't speak.

He shifted on his chair. He was too big for it. It wasn't the kind of chair made for lounging, but the only other option was to invite him to join her on the bed and no way on God's green was she doing that. The last time they'd been in bed together...

It had been heaven.

Once the thought flitted into her mind, it lodged there—a stubborn, sensual reminder that pecked at her, teased her. All the sensations Alex had created in her with deft fingers and a teasing mouth, with the dark appreciation of his eyes and intakes of breath as she'd explored his body with as much thoroughness as he'd explored hers—exquisite, torturous reminders—they all flooded through her now and her body instantly came alive in some kind of primal response. She recalled with startling accuracy the taste of him, the feel of him against her tongue, her palms...his scent. The way he'd—

'Kit!'

She jerked out of the recollection to find herself leaning towards Alex, breathing hard. Her name had scraped out of his mouth on a half-strangled choke. He was breathing as hard as her.

Oh, dear Lord! She wanted to close her eyes. She'd been

staring at him, practically *undressing* him with her eyes and begging him to—

And his eyes had darkened in response. She swallowed. She'd recognized the answering hunger that had stretched across his face before it had been comprehensively snapped off from her view.

He shot out of his chair and pretended to adjust the blind. She knew he was giving them both time to pull themselves together again, but she couldn't help noticing his hands weren't any steadier than hers.

How could it be like this? How could she want him so badly when she didn't even like him? How could he want her, knowing she was pregnant? She'd seen what the news of her pregnancy had done to him.

But he did want her. She read that too clearly to mistake it for anything else.

He raked a hand back through his hair. 'I picked you up some magazines while I was out.' He spoke to the window, not to her.

'Thank you.' She breathed a sigh of gratitude. Her voice was low, but at least it worked.

He finally turned. 'I thought if you wanted I could haul your television in here and set it up so you at least have something to watch.'

She shook her head. 'That's not necessary.' It'd only mean setting it back up out in the living room when she was well again. She suddenly frowned. Had too much sleep fogged her brain? 'Alex, why are you still here? Don't you have a company to run?'

'The company isn't important.'

She stilled at that, glanced down at the photo frame. Had he changed his mind about having a baby? Yesterday he'd been in shock and denial. But maybe today... 'Are you trying to tell me that you've come around to the idea of being a father?'

'No.' The single word was inflexible. His face had gone impassive, emotionless. It was an expression she was starting to recognize, and loathe.

'Then don't you think it would be better for both of us if you just left?'

He didn't say anything.

'Between them, Caro and Doreen can take perfectly good care of me.'

He dragged a hand down his face then before seizing the chair and pulling it back a foot or so and planting himself in it. He leant forward to rest his elbows on his knees. 'Caro told me that over the course of the next two days Doreen is booked in for a rash of tests at the hospital. It's something to do with late onset diabetes,' he added quickly when she bolted upright, 'and it's nothing serious, but...'

But it meant Doreen wouldn't be available to look after her. Kit settled back again, chewing her lip.

'And Doreen told me that Caro's mother is arriving from England tomorrow and—'

'Oh!' Kit clapped a hand to her forehead. 'Caro is collecting her from Sydney Airport. She's leaving at the crack of dawn to get there in time. I forgot.'

'She was going to change her plans and make other arrangements for her mother, but I told her not to. If you think I did wrong, then I can call her now and—'

'No, no. Caro hasn't seen her mum in over a year.' And while Caro's mother was staying for a month, Kit certainly wasn't going to be responsible for delaying their reunion.

'And we've all been trying to ring your grandmother,' Alex continued, 'but...'

Kit smiled faintly. 'But she's a gadabout who refuses

to carry a mobile phone. If you leave her a message on Tuesday you might hear back by Friday.'

'And your mother lives—'

'In Brisbane,' she finished for him.

She pressed her fingers to her temples. *Think!*

'Kit?'

She glanced up.

'I'm staying in Tuncurry until the weekend.'

'But—'

'It's non-negotiable. There are things we need to discuss, but they can wait until you are well again. It's just as easy for me to stay here and keep an eye on you than it is to book into a motel.'

Easy for who?

'And it's the least I can do.'

She sagged into her pillows, suddenly unutterably weary. 'What do you mean?'

'I know I hurt you, Kit.'

She wanted to look away, but those dark eyes of his held hers and something whispered between them. The memory of soaring together for one unforgettable night and touching the stars. No matter how much she wanted to deny it, this man had touched her soul. In that moment she recognized that she'd touched his too.

It didn't mean they had a future together, though. She saw that just as clearly.

'I hurt you, Kit, and I know I'm disappointing you now.' He rested his head in his hands for a brief moment. 'Knowing me has made your life worse. I can't begin to tell you how sorry I am about that.'

She blinked and then frowned. He looked as if he actually meant that.

'Helping you out for the next two and a half days is the least I can do.'

Two and a half days? When he put it like that, it didn't sound like much. And, frankly, there was no one else available because she had no intention whatsoever of imposing on either Caro or Doreen.

'Don't you think your baby's welfare is more important than anything else at the moment?'

'Yes,' she whispered. She did. With all her heart.

'So do I.'

She blinked and frowned. He did?

'So why don't we just do what the doctor ordered—you rest and I'll be general dogsbody?'

She drew in a breath. What he was proposing, she may not like it, but it made sense. She let out the breath in an unsteady whoosh. 'Okay, Alex.' She nodded. 'It seems to be the best solution. And…um…thank you.'

'No thanks necessary,' he said roughly.

She frowned suddenly, hitched up her chin. 'But you know what? Regardless of what you think, being pregnant, that hasn't made my life worse. Having a baby is wonderful.'

He turned grey. She shrugged. 'I just want you to know that you don't have to feel guilty about that. At least, not on my account.'

If he really did mean to walk away from his child, though, she hoped guilt would plague him every day of his sorry life.

He moved to fiddle with her CD player on the other side of the room. The sound of lapping water and soft squeals and gurgles filled the room.

She stared at him when he turned back around and then at the CD player. 'What on earth is that?'

'It's called *Sounds of the Sea*.' He shrugged and held up the CD case. 'It's supposed to be calming and relaxing.'

He'd bought her a relaxation CD!

'I got it from one of those hippy places when I went shopping earlier.' He rubbed the back of his neck and didn't quite meet her eyes. 'You know the doctor said you needed to relax. I thought the CD...'

'I thought you went shopping for a change of clothes, a toothbrush.'

'I did. And for food—your refrigerator was practically empty!'

'There are plenty of frozen TV dinners.' She shrugged at his stare. 'I don't cook.'

He planted his legs, hands on hips. 'What do you mean, you don't cook?'

She waved her hands in front of her face. 'This is all beside the point. Alex, you're doing my head in!'

One corner of his mouth kinked up. 'I'd appreciate it if you didn't mention that to Caro.'

The silence between them filled with the laughter of dolphins—oddly hypnotic. She shook herself out from under its spell. He might find this amusing, but she'd lost her sense of humour. There was too much at stake for laughing. Her baby...

'I just don't get you at all. You wanted me to terminate my pregnancy—'

'No, I didn't! I—'

'You threw up when I told you I was pregnant but now you're doing everything you can to make sure the baby stays healthy.'

He was silent for a moment. 'You want this baby, Kit. You've already given your heart to it. You love it. I would never take that away from you.'

Her chest clenched. Frustration, remembered joy and then the ensuing crushing desolation, Alex's generosity as a lover and then his callousness the next day, it all rose up through her now. She didn't understand him at all and yet she'd agreed to let him stay in her house.

She was having his baby!

She needed to understand at least some of what had happened between them or...

Or she'd have learned nothing.

'You were the most incredible lover, Alex, generous and thoughtful. You made me feel beautiful and cherished.' And loved, which just went to show how skewed her judgement had been.

He leapt up, going white at her words.

'And then the next day you acted as if what had happened between us meant nothing. No, even less that that, as if what had happened between us was an aberration.' She lifted her hands. 'Why?'

'It wouldn't have been fair to let you think we had a future.'

'But you were so utterly cold, so callous. You didn't even bother trying to let me down gently. What did I do wrong? Please—I don't ever want to make that same mistake again.' She had a baby to think of. Her heart jammed in her throat. What if next time it wasn't just her heart she broke but her child's too? If her judgement about him could be so off, how could she ever trust it again?

'How could you have changed so completely? What was that all about? Was it you? Or did I do something?' She couldn't hold the questions back. Her voice rose as each one burst from her. 'Why?'

Alex's face twisted in an emotion she couldn't identify— anger? Panic? Horror? He thrust an arm towards her stomach. *'Because I didn't want that!'*

The shouted words reverberated in the quiet of her cool, shady bedroom. They pulsed in the air like live things. Her hands crept across her stomach in an attempt to block her unborn baby's ears. In an attempt to protect it from pain and hurt. In an effort to console it. Her knees drew up beneath the covers to form a barrier between him and her.

'You really don't want this baby, do you?' She'd known that before, but now she knew it in a harder, more real way. And it hurt. It died, that part of her that hadn't been able to give up hope. Hope that once he'd recovered from the initial shock he'd come around, perhaps even welcome this baby into his life.

Alex was never going to accept this child.

'I'm sorry.' He'd gone a hideous kind of grey. 'I shouldn't have yelled.'

Perhaps not, but she couldn't really blame him. She'd pushed him. She hadn't meant to, it had just happened. But now she had her answer.

He dragged a hand back through his hair, eyed her uncertainly. 'Time for us to get calm again.'

'I am calm.'

Strangely enough, that was true. She felt icily and preternaturally calm. It didn't stop her from suspecting she may well cry buckets over all this later. 'I'm tired,' she whispered.

'I'll leave you to rest.'

CHAPTER SIX

On Wednesday evening Kit woke to the smell of something divine coming from the kitchen.

Alex poked his head around her bedroom door as if he had some finely tuned radar that let him know when she was awake. 'How are you feeling?'

'Good, thank you. Actually, really good.' Back-to-normal good. She pushed herself into a sitting position and smiled when her back proved totally pain-free. 'I can't believe how much I'm sleeping, though.'

'Your body needs the rest.' He shuffled his feet, glanced away. 'Dinner will be ready in five if you need to...' He waved towards the bathroom.

'Freshen up?' she supplied.

'Uh, right.'

No sooner had she made it back to bed and settled the covers around her when Alex walked in with a tray. Kit groaned as he set it on her lap. 'This smells heavenly.'

'It's just a beef and potato salad.'

She could tell he was pleased, though. She speared a piece of beef, popped it into her mouth and closed her eyes in bliss as she chewed.

When she opened her eyes she found Alex frozen to the spot, his eyes glued to her mouth. Her stomach, skin, even her ears, all tightened. 'I...um...' She cleared her throat and tried to tamp down on the heat rising through her. She set her fork to her plate before she dropped it, and searched her mind for something to say. 'You're…um… not going to eat out there on your own, are you?'

He snapped back. 'I thought—'

'Bring your plate in here, Alex. Do you know how boring it is being confined to bed?' And then she wondered if that was such a good idea. She didn't really want to spend more time in Alex's company than she had to, did she?

'It's only for one more day.'

'Half a day,' she corrected.

He stood for a moment as if undecided before leaving the room and returning with his plate. He settled himself on his chair.

She should get a nice little tub chair for this room. It was the last thought she was aware of thinking before she returned to her food. She couldn't believe how ravenous she was, and how much better she was feeling. She scraped up the last of the sauce with a piece of lettuce, chewed in avid appreciation and finally set her tray aside. 'That was unbelievably delicious. Though you didn't have to go to any trouble, you know?'

'No trouble.'

She didn't believe that for a moment. 'You could've just tossed a TV dinner into the microwave and I'd have been grateful for that.'

He polished off the last of his food too and set his plate on her dressing table. 'I can't believe you don't cook.'

'It's boring and messy and takes too long.'

'It doesn't have to be any of those things.'

'I do other things. I can crochet. That's nice and domestic.'

'You have a baby on the way. You need to know how to cook.'

Yes, she had a baby on the way. *His baby.* Only he didn't want anything to do with it.

An awkward silence opened up between them, turning her tongue to lead.

Alex cleared his throat. 'Finished?'

'Yes, thank you.'

'Would you like some more?'

'No, thank you.'

Her hands clenched in the quilt when he left with their empty plates. *Why was he still here!*

He returned a short while later with two mugs of steaming tea. He handed her one and settled himself on the seat at the end of her bed again.

'So.' He cleared his throat. He didn't look any more at ease than she did. 'This is where you grew up?'

She took a careful sip and then nodded. 'The house where I grew up is a few blocks closer to the river.'

'And you have lots of friends here, lots of honorary aunts and uncles?'

Was he trying to reassure himself that she had backup for when he did leave? Was that what all this was about? Him staying here looking after her—was it his attempt to assuage a guilty conscience?

No, no, he was too ruthless for that.

She bit her lip. He'd framed her ultrasound photo.

He'd bought her a relaxation CD.

Maybe he had a *seriously* guilty conscience?

'Kit?'

She shook herself, searched and found the thread of their conversation again. 'This was a great place to grow up. Doreen next door used to be the school secretary at my old primary school and what she doesn't know about my old classmates isn't worth knowing.'

He grimaced and she could see how this small-community lifestyle might seem suffocating to him, but she wasn't going to lie about the kind of life she wanted for herself and her baby. 'I barely clapped eyes on my neighbours in Sydney.' Everybody was too busy working long hours, dealing with long commutes into the CBD. 'I like knowing my neighbours' names. I like chatting over the back fence. I like knowing that they're keeping an eye on me and that I can do the same for them.'

She had no regrets about leaving the busy pace of the city behind.

'Auntie Doreen is a good friend of my grandmother's. My grandma used to live across the street.' Which was probably why she'd jumped at the chance to buy this house. The street held good memories for her.

Alex frowned. 'She doesn't live there now, though, does she?'

Her eyes narrowed. 'No, Alex, she doesn't. I'd have sent you to sit on her veranda to wait till she'd returned home from wherever it was she'd been, so it could be her rather than you sitting here talking to me right now.'

'I didn't mean…'

'She moved into a retirement village in Forster five years ago when my mother relocated to Brisbane. She delights in all the activity the village offers. She has a very full social life.' Before he could ask, she added, 'Forster is across the bridge.' Forster and Tuncurry were twin townships separated from each other by the channel of water that fed into Wallis Lake.

Did he really mean to abandon his child? As the question speared into her, an ache stretched behind her eyes, pounding in time to her pulse.

'You look tired again. I should let you get more rest.'

He went to take her mug but she kept hold of it, forcing him to look at her. His fingers felt cool against hers.

Unbidden, images of what he'd done with those fingers rose up through her. She snatched her hand away. She didn't know how he managed to keep hold of the mug or prevent its dregs from spilling over her quilt. All she knew was that she couldn't think when he touched her.

'What the—'

Whatever he saw in her face had him biting back the rest of his words. His jaw had clenched so hard she suspected he wouldn't be able to utter them now anyway.

'I want to ask you something.' She was appalled at her uneven breathiness. She'd wanted to sound cool, calm and in control. Unflappable.

Where Alex was concerned, though, she was highly flappable. And flammable!

His choked out, 'Ask what?' didn't help either. She knew precisely how flammable he could be.

He didn't meet her eyes. The pulse at the base of his jaw jumped and jerked.

She stared down at her hands to find her fingers mechanically pleating the quilt.

Alex reached out and trapped them beneath his hand, stilling them. 'Kit, just tell me what's on your mind.'

He sat back down and just like that some of the tension eased out of her. She pulled in one long, hard breath. 'You said you weren't leaving Tuncurry until we'd sorted out a few things. I want to know what those things are.'

'There'll be time enough for that once you've received the all-clear from the doctor tomorrow.'

She could almost see him replay the doctor's words through his mind. *No stress, no worry.*

She folded her arms. 'Look, I'm going to worry about this until we sort it out. Either you let me stew about it all night or we can talk now.'

For a moment she thought he was going to refuse, get

up and walk away. 'Can we keep this calm?' he finally asked instead.

'We're adults, aren't we?' she countered.

He surveyed her for a long moment. It took a concerted effort not to fidget under those dark inscrutable eyes. 'Okay, Kit.' He nodded. 'Once the child is born I want a paternity test carried out. If the child is mine then I'll arrange for child support payments.'

She kept her voice perfectly polite. 'No.'

He leant forward. 'What do you mean, no? I have every right to demand a paternity test.'

'Really?' Even though she'd steeled herself for this, she was still surprised at how much his distrust hurt. 'Just for argument's sake, let's say that we do get the test done and you discover that the baby is yours, and, believe me, Alex, that is what you'll find out. But once you have incontrovertible proof, what is it going to change? Are you going to want visitation rights? Are you going to be a *real* father to this baby?'

He turned ashen. 'No, but I'll at least make sure that financially you and the baby are taken care of.'

'You can take your blood money and sod off, Alex!' She abandoned all pretence at politeness. 'I can look after this baby on my own—financially and otherwise.'

'It is my duty to provide financial support. It's a legal requirement.'

'It's your duty to be a proper father, but it's obvious that moral requirements don't figure on your radar! So you can take your legal requirements and stuff them up your shirt for all I care.'

She wanted to drop her head to her knees and weep for her unborn child.

'I can't believe you're prepared to turn your back like

that on your own child, Alex. And I can't believe that you could accuse me of lying about this, of—'

'I'm not accusing you of anything!'

'Yes, you are!'

He swore, scrubbed both hands down his face. 'Hell, Kit, this isn't about you.'

'Not about me? How can you—'

'I've been lied to once before.'

The world tilted to one side for a moment before righting itself again. Kit moistened her lips. When she could speak again she asked, 'When? Who…?' Who would do such a thing?

'My ex-wife.'

Her own hurt vanished. Just like that.

His face had gone unreadable, impassive. She suddenly found that she wanted to cry for him too. 'What happened?'

He dropped his head to his hands. For a long moment Kit didn't think he'd answer. Finally, he dragged both hands down his face and straightened. 'Jacqueline and I had been married for fifteen months when she fell pregnant. She told me the baby was mine and I had no reason to doubt her. We'd dated for over a year before we married.'

He'd loved a woman once, enough to marry her? She rubbed at her arms but it couldn't erase the sting that bloomed across her skin.

His mouth tightened. 'It never occurred to me that she'd lie. And God help me, but when I found out she was pregnant I couldn't wait to hold my son. We called him Chad.'

Kit's spine lost all its strength. Her hands crept up to cover her mouth. Before her eyes, Alex aged. His skin lost its colour. The lines around his mouth and eyes grew more pronounced. Shadows took up residence in his eyes. She

dragged her hands back down to her lap, gripped them together. 'When did you find out the truth?'

'Not until Chad was two.'

Her mouth went dry. Alex had spent two years, not
to mention the nine months of the pregnancy, loving his
son—his Chad—and giving his heart to him completely?
He didn't have to say that out loud—the evidence was
written in every line of his body, in the grief that twisted
his mouth and made his shoulders slump.

'Oh, Alex! What happened?'

'She took him away.'

She had to gulp back a sob at the raw pain in his voice.

'She had paternity tests carried out and they proved that
I...'

'But you'd raised him. You loved him!' The words burst
from her. 'Alex, you must've had rights.'

'She and her lover—Chad's biological father—left before I'd gathered my wits. They fled to South America.'

Kit stared at him. No! This episode in his life—it
couldn't end like this. Alex had loved that little boy. That
little boy would've loved Alex.

'The legal advice I received wasn't promising. After
all, what legal rights did I really have?' His face twisted.
'Oh, I had the money to drag the case through the courts
for years, but in the end who would I really be hurting?'

Chad. The knowledge sucked the air out of her lungs.
He'd done what was best for the little boy he loved, but it
hadn't given him an ounce of comfort. It had left a deep
and lasting scar.

'Don't cry for me, Kit.'

It wasn't until he reached across to brush her tears away
with the pad of his thumb that she realized she was crying.

'I'm not worth it.'

Wasn't he? Suddenly she wasn't so sure.

'Because the fact is, no matter what I tell myself, I can't go through that again.'

A weight settled in the middle of her chest.

'I once had a son, Kit, and now I don't. So you see, the paternity test, it isn't about you, it's about me. If your child is mine I will do what is legally required, but nothing more.'

CHAPTER SEVEN

ALEX strode out to the dark of the back garden and tried to draw air into his lungs.

He hadn't meant to tell Kit about Chad. He didn't talk about Chad. To anyone.

His gut clenched. He strode down to the back fence to wrap his fingers around the hard bark of the banksia tree until they started to burn and ache. He hadn't realized how much Kit's inability to fathom his previous treatment of her had plagued her, tormented her, had her questioning her own judgement and doubting herself. His mouth filled with acid. This was why he should have been more careful in the first place—resisted the temptation she'd presented, the lure of a life that he knew could never be his. But her sunshine had touched his soul, and for a short time he had been lost.

And she'd paid the price.

He'd wanted—needed—to reassure her that none of this was her fault. The only way to do that was to tell her about Chad. To tell her why he couldn't go through all that again.

Her unborn child—it was a source of joy for her.

For him... For him it was a constant source of torment, reminding him of everything he'd had and then lost, re-minding him of the gaping hole at the centre of himself that nothing could fill. In losing Chad he'd lost the best part of himself.

If there'd ever been a best part of himself.

He didn't want another child.

He didn't want to *love* another child.

He'd given Chad everything—his time, his care, all the love in his heart. But it hadn't been enough. Jacqui had still left. He'd still lost the child he loved.

He wasn't going through that a second time.

Losing Chad had proved something that deep down he'd always known but had never wanted to believe—he didn't have what it took to be a family man. He refused to hide from the hard facts now. He could not give Kit what she so badly wanted—a stable and loving family unit.

What was the point in trying when he'd only lose it all again anyway?

Not hiding from the hard facts again? He gave a mirthless laugh. His demand for a paternity test was a lie, a blind, an excuse to hide behind. Kit wasn't lying. Her baby was his. He just didn't want to believe it, that was all. Kit didn't care about his money and she sure as hell didn't see him as a great catch. She'd prefer it if he *wasn't* her baby's father.

He rested his head against the trunk of the tree. Jacqui had taken Chad away from him without a backward glance. There were no guarantees that Kit wouldn't do the same. Eventually.

He would not relive that nightmare. Not for Kit. Not for anyone. If that made him a monster in her eyes, then so be it.

He loosened his grip on the tree to glance around the garden, which was partially illuminated by the light from the kitchen window. His gaze fell on the Cape Cod chair that Kit had been sanding the other day.

Do something useful.

He strode towards it. His mind worked best when his fingers were busy, and tonight he needed his mind to be at its peak.

Because, no matter what he told himself, he couldn't just up and leave when the weekend rolled around. He might not be able to offer Kit emotional support, but he couldn't abandon her with a house threatening to fall down around her ears either. Not when she was expecting a baby. He had to come up with a plan she'd go for and fast.

Because if he didn't, once she received the all clear from her doctor tomorrow he may well find himself very politely thanked and very firmly asked to leave. And who'd make sure she had everything she needed then?

Kit woke early on Thursday morning. She tried to go back to sleep but the nerves leaping and jumping in her stomach wouldn't let her.

Today she'd have her scan. Today she'd find out if her baby was okay.

A tap sounded on her bedroom door and Alex's head poked around its corner. How did he always know when she was awake?

'Good morning.'

She swallowed. He looked fresh and alert and good enough to eat. She pushed up against the pillows, dragged her hands back over her hair, tried to smooth it. 'Morning.'

'How are you feeling?'

'Fine.' Physically in herself, she was. She felt as if she'd never been sick in the first place.

But what if her high temperature had harmed her baby? What then? She knew worrying about that would do her no good, but not worrying was impossible.

Alex's eyes narrowed. 'Breakfast?'

She shook her head. She doubted she'd be able to keep anything down. 'A cup of something hot and herbal would be great, though.' Despite what the doctor had said, she'd given up caffeine the day she'd found out she was pregnant. She'd wanted to give her baby every chance.

Alex appeared with two mugs of…lemongrass tea. The fragrance made her stomach loosen a fraction. She accepted her mug with a lift of the lips that she hoped would pass for a smile. 'You do know that I don't mind if you drink coffee, don't you? You don't need to abstain just because I am.'

'It doesn't seem fair to drink it when you can't. Besides, this lemon stuff is halfway decent.' His nose wrinkled. 'But you can keep that chamomile nonsense to yourself.'

She found herself chuckling, even amidst all the anxiety swirling through her.

'Nervous, huh?'

She didn't know how he'd sensed it. She'd thought she'd done a good job at covering it up. It seemed pointless trying to deny it, though. 'A little.'

He surveyed her for a moment, set his mug on the floor and then leaned towards her. 'Your temperature came down very quickly, Kit. You've had lots of rest, good food and medicine. You're young, strong and the picture of health again. There's no reason to believe that your baby isn't strong and healthy too.'

She nodded. She knew he was right.

'But?' he said softly.

She set her mug on the bedside table as her stomach clenched up again. 'Do you believe in fate, Alex?'

'Not really.'

He didn't pick his mug up again. He remained with elbows on knees, his full attention focused on her. For a moment it made her feel spotlighted—at the centre of his world. She shook herself.

'Why?' he asked.

She swallowed again, found her fingers had started pleating and unpleating the quilt. She gripped them together to still them. 'Maybe I'm not fated to be a mother. I didn't realize I was pregnant for three whole months. I drank caffeine and the occasional glass of wine, and…and I didn't do stuff that I would've done had I known.'

He frowned. 'Kit, you're going to be just fine.'

'Fine?' Her voice rose. 'How on earth can you say that? On Monday I didn't even realize I was sick! Honestly, Alex, what does that say about me and the kind of mother I'm going to make?' Her heart ached. She pressed her palms to her eyes for a moment before dragging them back into her lap. 'It doesn't reflect very well on me, does it? For heaven's sake, I don't even know how to change a nappy! Maybe…' She gulped. 'Maybe I'm not meant to be a mother.'

'What the hell…? No!'

Alex jumped up, knocking over his mug in the process. With a swift curse he tore off his T-shirt and used it to mop up the spill.

As a broad expanse of naked flesh met her gaze, Kit's eyes went wide. She could feel them getting bigger and bigger as the space in her lungs for air became progressively smaller and smaller. Her thought processes slammed to a halt. Alex's shoulders and chest and the sculpted line of his back—tanned, muscled and toned—all beckoned to her. She knew from experience how firm his skin would be to the touch. And how warm.

Her pulse skittered and skipped and skated through her veins.

'Didn't want the rug to stain,' he said, his voice gruff as he glanced up at her.

She sucked her bottom lip into her mouth, felt an answering tug in her womb as he rose to his feet and stood before her in all his half-naked glory. She remembered another time... Her stomach, her lips, her limbs softened.

Oh, dear Lord! She tried to catch her breath. 'I...um... You didn't need to ruin your shirt in the process.'

He lifted one powerful shoulder as he sat again, the T-shirt hanging negligently from his hands. 'I'll throw it in the wash later. It'll be fine.'

The muscular definition of his biceps and the sinewy strength of his forearms had her melting against the bedclothes. He was so tanned. Had he worked beneath a hot African sun without his shirt?

'You're going to be a great mother, Kit.'

That dragged her attention back. His eyes had darkened to coal and they stared at her intensely as if by their very force they could compel her to believe his words.

'What makes you so sure?' she whispered. She wanted to believe him—desperately—but...

'Look at how much effort you're going to in order to provide your baby with the best life you can. You've moved back to this place that you love because you think it's a good place to raise your child. You've bought a house and you're getting it ready for your baby's arrival. You're surrounding your baby with a community of people who will love it almost as much as you will.'

She bit her lip.

'Kit?'

She glanced up into those coal-dark eyes again.

'You love your baby. That's more important than knowing how to change a nappy or abstaining from caffeine or...or anything! You want to be a mother, right?'

She nodded.

'Then you're going to be just fine. You'll learn all the things you need to know about being a mum along the way. You have your family and friends and your baby books to help you. You'll probably make the odd mistake because you're human like the rest of us, but it won't mean you love your baby any less and it won't make you a bad person. It certainly won't make you a bad mother.'

She blinked, considered his words, and then sent him a shaky smile. 'You're right. Thank you. I'm sorry, I just panicked for a bit.'

'Nothing to apologise for.'

He leaned back in his seat. It highlighted the flatness of his stomach and the way the muscles there coiled and flexed beneath his skin. Her gaze drifted downwards and she noted how the waistband of his jeans sat low on his hips. Her mouth and throat went dry.

'There's something I'd like to discuss with you, Kit. I was going to wait until after your doctor's appointment, but that's still hours away.'

She sensed that he wanted to distract her from brooding on her worries about her baby's health. She started to lift her eyes, wanted to thank him again for easing her fears, but his chest and shoulders proved more of a distraction than his words. His chest started to rise and fall with a rhythm that matched hers. Her fingers clenched in the quilt. A pulse pounded at the base of his throat. Firm, lean lips opened. Heat swirled through her.

That magnificent body leapt up. Kit's breath caught and she started to lean towards him—

'I'll be back in a moment.'

The words—hoarse with need—scraped out of his throat and caressed all the hairs on her arms into lifting as if in surrender. He surged out of her room, the muscles in his back rippling, and Kit melted back into her pillows, her mind too fuzzed to work.

He returned a moment later, dragging another shirt on over his head.

Heat of an entirely different variety burned her cheeks, her face, her throat then. She wanted to cover her head with the bedclothes. Instead she buried her face in her lukewarm mug of tea while Alex opened the bedroom window wider to let in the cool morning air and then busied himself with her CD player. *Sounds of the Sea* filtered into the room. He kept his back to her and she wondered if he was having as much trouble getting himself under control as she was.

Eventually she managed to clear her throat. 'You wanted to talk to me about something?'

He turned then, moved his chair another foot or so away from her bed. If he kept doing that he'd end up in the bathroom.

He sat. 'That's right, I did.'

'Well?' she prompted when he didn't continue.

'Kit, do you have a job lined up yet?'

She stared. A job? And then she rolled her eyes. 'You don't need to worry about my finances. I had a very nice nest egg squirreled away before I left Sydney.'

'Enough to cover expensive repairs on your house?'

She bit her lip and glanced away. She could get a bank loan.

When you don't have a job. Ha! Fat chance.

Her stomach clenched and her pulse started to race. She'd better start job-hunting asap because she needed the house ready for when the baby came. She glanced back at Alex. She'd failed in providing her baby with a father. She couldn't fail on this too. Alex had calmed her fears about her ability to be a good mother, but to prove she could be a good parent she had to get this house, and her life, on track fast. Finding a job was the first place to start.

'Kit, I want to barter an exchange of labour with you.'

'A…' She stilled. 'Why?'

'Because I think it would be to both our benefits.'

An exchange of labour?

'I'd really like you to finish that book project for McBride's.'

'Alex—' she lifted her hands and then let them drop again '—there are any number of people at Hallam Enterprises more than capable of finishing that project. Didn't you read my report?'

'It was *your* passion that had that book offer tabled to us in the first place. It was *your* passion that sold me on the deal. It's *your* passion that will make it a success.'

'Your name on the cover will do that—your experience, your expertise.'

'I can't write the thing, though. You're the one who translates all that so-called experience and expertise into a compelling, readable account. That's where your expertise lies. We make a good team, Kit.'

She stilled at his words. A team—her and Alex?

'I want you to finish overseeing the work on the book because you are the best person for the job. With an Internet connection here you can work remotely. You won't need to go into the office.'

'You said a barter of labour. What will you be doing?'

'Fixing your house.'

Her jaw dropped. 'Alex, you've just returned from a month abroad. You can't afford to take more time off work.'

His chin tilted at an arrogant angle. 'It's my company. I can do what I want. Besides, Donald has everything under control in the Sydney office.' He shrugged and the arrogance vanished behind the beginnings of a smile. A wry smile admittedly, but potent for all that. 'He's doing a good job and I am only a phone call away if there's an emergency.'

'But...' Her mind wouldn't work.

'I'll fix the hole in your roof and the hole in your wall. I'll repoint the piers on the southern side of the house and replace the guttering. I'll check for dry rot and—' his lips twisted '—not-so-dry rot. I'll modernise the bathroom and give the whole place a lick of paint, inside and out.'

Her eyes widened as his list grew. Whatever he saw in her face made him leap to his feet and stalk over to the window, hands shoved deep into his pockets.

She moistened her lips. 'It sounds as if I'm getting the better end of that deal.'

'Financially you'd be better off if you stayed on the books at Hallam Enterprises, took the maternity leave you'd be entitled to, and paid a builder to make the repairs.'

She needed a job *and* she needed the house ready for when the baby came. Alex was offering her both in one fell swoop. He didn't want to be a father, but he didn't want to leave her in the lurch. That much was clear.

Maybe the truth of the matter was that Alex couldn't walk away from his child and he just hadn't realized that yet.

She remembered the expression on his face when he'd talked about Chad. He had glowed with love, his face soft with it, before the anguish had taken over. He'd wanted a child once.

She lifted her chin. 'Will you help me decorate the nursery?'

He shuffled his feet, rolled his shoulders. His lips turned down but his chin didn't drop. 'Consider it added to the list.'

'Then, Alex Hallam, we have ourselves a deal.'

'Excellent!'

Just for a moment, his smile bathed her in light.

'Ready for breakfast yet?'

'Yes, please.' Suddenly she found she was ravenous.

The doctor unwrapped the blood pressure monitor from around her arm. 'I'm delighted to say you're as fit as a fiddle.'

To her left she was aware of Alex sagging in his chair. Relief? She wouldn't be privy to that particular emotion until after the scan. She gripped her hands together and prayed her illness hadn't harmed her baby in any way.

'I'd like you to keep taking it easy for a bit, though. Rest when you get tired. You also need to make sure you finish the course of antibiotics.'

She could practically see Alex file those instructions away in case he needed to bring them out and wave them under her nose and recite 'doctor's orders' at her. It made her feel looked after, cared for, as if someone had her back. It was why she hadn't kicked up a fuss when he'd accompanied her into the doctor's consulting room. He'd looked after her so comprehensively these past few days. Besides, this was his baby too. He deserved to know if it was healthy and developing normally.

'Okay, let's do the scan. Jump up onto the table.' The doctor gestured to an examination table.

Alex leapt to his feet, paled. 'I'll…um…wait outside.'

'Alex, no!' Kit grabbed his hand, her stomach twisting and her heart pounding. If the news wasn't good she didn't think she could face it on her own. His mouth whitened. His shoulders clenched, but he didn't shake his hand free from her grip. Eventually he nodded.

'Thank you,' she whispered. She tried to release his

hand, but found that she couldn't. Finally he smiled, just a slight drawing up on the right side of his mouth, but it helped ease some of the tension that had her wrapped up tight.

'C'mon, Kit, up onto the table.'

He helped her up onto it, which was just as well because her legs had turned to putty. He held her hand when the doctor squirted cold gel onto her stomach.

'There's your baby, Kit.'

Kit's gaze shot to the monitor. 'Is it okay? Did my high temperature—'

'Your baby is perfect.'

She closed her eyes and sent up a prayer of thanks.

'Everything looks exactly as it should,' the doctor continued. 'Your temperature came down very quickly. I can't envisage any problems. Look, here's the head…an arm.'

Her body went loose and light as relief, joy and gratitude all flooded through her. She turned to grin up at Alex, to share her joy, but Alex wasn't looking at her, he was staring at the screen. At the picture of their baby. And just for a moment hunger stretched across his face. It thickened her throat. It made her want to throw her arms around him.

And then he went pale. Perspiration beaded his forehead, his top lip.

'Would you like to know the sex of your baby?'

Alex dropped her hand, he backed up and then he bolted from the room. A chill settled over her. She tried to blink the sting from her eyes.

'Kit?' the doctor queried softly.

She stared back at the screen and shook her head. 'I… uh…think I'd like that to be a surprise.'

He nodded and let her stare at the screen for a bit longer.

'You know what the pregnancy books say, don't you?' he finally said.

It took a force of will to focus on the doctor's words rather than the doubts cascading through her mind. 'What's that?'

'A woman becomes a mother the moment she finds out she's pregnant. A man becomes a father only when his child is placed in his arms.'

She moistened her lips. Could he be right?

Her heart burned. She had a feeling it would take a miracle for Alex to embrace fatherhood again.

Then she recalled the hunger that had stretched across his face. Maybe it wasn't a miracle they needed, just some time?

She fastened her jeans again, thanked the doctor and left the consulting room to find Alex pacing in the corridor. Without a word, he took her arm and led her outside to the car. He opened the passenger door for her, but she didn't duck inside. She stood her ground until he met her eyes. 'I'm sorry I put you through that. I'm sorry I asked you to stay when it quite obviously brought back bad memories for you.'

'You have nothing to apologise for, Kit.' His voice was clipped and short. 'I'm just glad that your baby is well.'

It's your baby too! she wanted to shout as he walked around to the driver's side.

She ducked inside the car and waited until he was seated beside her. 'If I'd known the scan would remind you of Chad I wouldn't have asked you to stay.'

He didn't say anything.

'The thing is—' she swallowed '—I wouldn't have thought the memory of Chad's scan would be a bad thing. I'd have thought it'd be a happy memory.'

'There is nothing happy to be had in any of those memories!'

She flinched at his tone, its hardness. 'I…I was afraid that the scan would show something bad. I couldn't face that on my own. Your being there, it helped…thank you.'

The pounding behind Alex's eyes intensified at Kit's simple words. Finding out her baby was well and healthy—it should have been a moment of joy for her. He'd ruined that.

But he hadn't been able to stay in that room a moment longer. His stomach had become a hard ball of anguish that he thought would split him in two. The picture on the screen and the sound of the baby's heartbeat had threatened to tear him apart.

A bead of perspiration detached itself from his nape to trickle all the way down his back.

That's not Kit's fault.

He closed his eyes and dragged in a breath, tried to grab the tatters of his control and shape them back into place around him. He would fix her house; he would make arrangements to pay her child support. He'd fulfil his obligations. And then he'd get the hell out of her life. He didn't have anything more to offer her.

He sent her a sidelong glance. She'd gone pale. The knowledge that he'd robbed her of her joy left a bitter taste in his mouth. He had to clench his hands on the steering wheel to stop from leaning forward and resting his head on it.

He started up the car because there wasn't anything else he could think to do. 'I thought we could do some shopping, do something about the woeful state of your freezer. I figured it was time someone taught you to cook.'

His attempt at levity didn't work.

'I don't much feel like shopping.'

Idiot! Why hadn't he been able to control his reaction to the scan? She'd been ill. She was still recovering. He was supposed to be looking out for her.

He opened his mouth to apologise, to explain, but the words wouldn't come. He revved the car extra hard. He shoved his shoulders back. 'You're right. It's time we got back. I'm expecting a delivery from the hardware store.'

The delivery had already arrived by the time they returned. The wood was neatly stacked in the front garden beneath a tarpaulin. Frank was in the process of stacking all the tools Alex had hired onto the veranda out of the weather.

He strode up to Alex and clapped him on the shoulder. 'Howdy, neighbour.'

The familiarity had him rolling his shoulders. 'Hello, Frank.' It took a concerted effort not to add, *I'm only here temporarily, you know?*

'What did the doctor say, Kitty-Kat?'

Kit lifted her chin and smiled at Frank with an easiness that made his heart burn. She hadn't smiled at him like that since he'd arrived in Tuncurry.

'I got the all-clear. Mother and baby are doing fine.'

'That's grand news, love.'

It was. And Alex had rained on her parade. He didn't deserve her smiles.

Frank gestured to the tools. 'Good to see you haven't wasted any time. What's the plan?'

Alex told him because it was easier than following Kit into the house and dealing with the reproachful silence she'd subjected him to in the car.

He'd deserved it, he knew that, but he didn't know how to put things right. It'd be better for all concerned if she just kept thinking of him as some kind of unfeeling monster.

He battled the scowl building up inside him and told Frank how he meant to replace the joists and wall studs in the living room wall after he'd fixed the broken tiles on the roof, and then how he was going to re-plaster the wall and paint the house.

'If you need a hand…'

Frank's eager face finally burned itself into his brain. Frank wanted to help, was dying to be useful, and Alex didn't have the heart to rain on another person's parade today. 'You wouldn't happen to be handy with a sander by any chance, would you?'

'I would be.'

Alex clapped the older man on the shoulder. 'Then you're hired. A second pair of hands will be a godsend.'

Frank beamed at him and Alex found he could still smile. After a fashion.

CHAPTER EIGHT

KIT and Alex spent the next week working on their individual projects. Because there was so much dust and noise from the work Alex was doing in the living-dining area, Kit had set up a temporary office in one corner of her bedroom—a card table, her laptop and a file that was over a foot thick that had been couriered from Sydney.

Alex always broke off at lunchtime to make sure she ate. And that Frank ate too, if the older man was helping and hadn't already left for one of his tri-weekly swims that Doreen insisted he keep up. 'Mondays, Wednesdays and Fridays, lovey. Doctor's orders.'

Kit had the distinct impression that some days Frank was more of a hindrance than a help. His pleasure at being of use, though, touched her. So did Alex's patience with him.

It was a side she hadn't seen to Alex before. As the multi-millionaire executive in Sydney, Alex had been demanding, dictatorial and, at times, difficult. He paid his executives top dollar and as a result he expected them to be on the ball—no excuses. But this Alex, the builder-tradesman working on her house in Tuncurry, he was more laid-back, more relaxed. More human.

He made her heart beat harder too.

Nonsense! Don't rhapsodise.

It was just…if Alex could be this good with an eager elderly gentleman, then wouldn't he be great with a child?

The thought hitched her breath, made her stomach churn and her fingers tremble. She pushed away from the card table to pace. She'd been lucky thus far in her pregnancy—she hadn't suffered much from nausea. But whenever she thought of Alex's reaction during her scan, her stomach rebelled and bile rose in her throat.

He had become so *dark*!

She paused in her pacing to pull both hands back through her hair. She couldn't deny it. She wanted a father for baby. Even a part-time father was better than no father at all. Before she'd found out about Chad, she'd thought Alex the lowest of low lifes. But now she knew he would never hurt their baby the way her father had hurt her.

She remembered all the nights as a child when she'd lain awake yearning for a father, the joy when he'd finally become a part of her life. The devastation when she'd found out how little she'd really meant to him.

Chad had meant the world to Alex. It didn't take a genius to figure that one out. Couldn't this baby mean the world to him too?

She swung away, hands clenched. It wasn't fair that her baby—*their* baby—be forced to suffer because of another's crimes. What was really holding Alex back from embracing fatherhood a second time? Did he think history would repeat itself?

She stumbled. Was that it? Did he think she would take his baby away from him the way his ex-wife had?

She turned to stare at the door. If that were the case… She bit her lip. She had to get him to un-think that as soon as she could.

* * *

Alex glanced around as Kit emerged from the hallway door and carefully closed it behind her. Keeping it closed kept the worst of the dust out of the bedrooms.

Last week, Alex had moved a camp bed and his clothes into the spare bedroom. The nursery. It shared a wall with Kit's bedroom. He wasn't sleeping well. One wall didn't seem like much of a barrier and at night, whenever he closed his eyes, all he could see was Kit's glorious nakedness. It made him ache and burn.

Just like her impersonal politeness made him ache and burn. He missed their easy-going banter, the connection that had once existed between them. Telling himself it was for the best didn't help.

Grinding his teeth together, he ordered himself to focus back on the sanding, but before he could he caught an eyeful of the way her breasts pressed against the cotton of her simple shirtdress and he found he could barely move let alone get back to work. Her curves had become curvier in the last few days and only a saint could deny noticing.

Both he and Kit knew he wasn't a saint.

Kit glanced behind him. 'Ooh, no hole!' She pointed and moved towards it.

'Don't touch. It's still wet.' He'd only just finished plastering it. He glanced back at her, tried to keep his eyes above neck level. 'How's your work coming along?'

Her lips turned down and he could've kicked himself for asking. He didn't want her thinking he was checking up on her or anything.

She wrinkled her nose. 'Slow.'

She thrust out one hip and surveyed him. Her legs went…all the way up. He gulped. She hadn't been wearing that dress at lunchtime. Just as well too. With the memory of that much bare skin on display he'd have made a mess of the wall.

'Wanna go fishing?'

That jerked his eyes back to her face. The beginnings of a smile played around the corners of her mouth. He'd do a lot to turn it into a full-blown smile.

'Fishing?'

She shrugged as if it was no skin off her nose whether he said yes or no, but that smile no longer threatened to come out and play.

He shifted his weight from one leg to the other and then back again. He should stay as far away from this woman as he could. 'I've never been fishing.'

She rolled her eyes. 'That's not what I asked. Would you like to give it a go?'

Did he? He didn't know. The thought of spending the rest of the afternoon skiving off with Kit sounded great. Too great if the truth be told. He should resist it, wrestle her house into shape and then get the hell out of here. 'Where?'

'On the breakwater.'

He stared at her blankly. Her hands flew to her hips. 'Alex Hallam, haven't you explored even the tiniest bit since you've been here? Haven't you had a look at the beaches or the lake or anything?'

He knew where the hardware store and the supermarket were. He didn't need to know anything else. Besides, he'd had too many other things on his mind—like Kit's pregnancy—to play tourist.

Garbage! All you've done is avoid thinking about Kit's pregnancy. In fact, he suspected he'd rather staple gun his hand to the wall than talk about pregnancy and babies.

So he'd concentrated all his efforts on her house instead.

Not on the fact that he was going to become a father.

And not on playing tourist.

In case Kit hadn't noticed, he wasn't precisely in holiday-maker mode.

She shook her head, almost in pity. 'C'mon, all work and no play is making Jill a *very* dull girl.'

She eyed him up and down. It made his skin go tight and hot. Her eyes skittered away and he watched as she swallowed once, twice. 'What you're wearing will do fine, unless you'd rather change into a pair of board shorts.'

He shook his head. She'd said fishing. Not swimming.

'Put that down.' She pointed to the sander. 'You can come and help me haul the fishing rods out of the garden shed. Chop-chop.'

He kicked himself into action. It was only one afternoon.

Alex parked his car and spent a moment just drinking in the view. Finally he turned to Kit. 'I had no idea it would be so beautiful.'

The grin she sent him warmed him as effectively as the sun on the bare flesh of his arms. She settled a floppy canvas hat on her head and gestured in the direction of the breakwater. 'C'mon.'

She insisted on carrying one of the fishing rods—the lightest one—and Alex carried the other rod, the tackle box, a bucket and the net. He couldn't explain the primal urge to take her rod, though, and add it to his load.

Perhaps it was just good manners?

Yeah, right! If he had any manners whatsoever he wouldn't be trying to catch as big an eyeful of those golden legs of hers as he could.

She pointed to their right. 'This is called the Rock Pool. It's where all the local kids learn to swim. It's where I learned to swim.'

A sweep of golden sand and clear water stretched out

from the breakwater to a smaller bank of rocks bordering the channel. Kit told him the channel led into Wallis Lake. The breakwater provided a wave trap and this little bay had been roped off to provide a safe place to swim. Tiny waves lapped at the shore in rhythmic whooshes and the water was so clear he could see the sandy bottom, free from rocks and seaweed. He couldn't think of a prettier place to learn to swim.

To their left, though, stretched mile upon mile of golden sand and the foaming, rolling breakers of a surf beach. The salt in the air and the sound of the breakers intensified the further they walked out on the breakwater. The firmness of the path beneath his feet, the warmth of the spring sun and the sound of seagulls on the breeze eased tension out of his shoulders he hadn't even known was there.

'Is that where you swam as a teenager?' He pointed to the surf beach. He'd bet at sixteen she'd been a golden surfer girl.

She grinned at him and it struck him that she still was.

'Sometimes. But when I was a teenager my friends and I hung out at Forster beach.' She waved her hand to her right, indicating somewhere across the channel. 'It was *way* cooler.'

He laughed at the teenage inflection. He paused to glance back at the bridge that spanned the channel and connected the two townships of Tuncurry and Forster. It was white and wooden and gleamed in the sun.

She nudged his arm and urged him forward again. 'C'mon, I want to see if my favourite rock is taken.'

She had a favourite rock?

It was a huge flat monstrosity about three-quarters of the way along the breakwater that looked as if it would comfortably hold four people with room to spare. She gave a whoop and immediately clambered down to it.

'Heck, Kit!' Alex tried to keep up with her, tried to put a hand under her elbow to steady her. An impossibility given his armful of fishing rod and tackle box. He dropped the bucket. 'Steady on. You're pregnant. You're supposed to take it easy.'

She turned back to look at him, hand on her head to keep her hat in place. 'It doesn't make me an infirm old granny, you know? Now, c'mon, front and centre. I'm going to teach you how to cast off and if you don't get the knack by your third go I'm going to push you in.'

The bark of laughter that shot out of him took him completely by surprise, but Kit's eyes were so bright with pleasure that he didn't try to suppress it.

He managed to cast off successfully on his second go. Kit cast off next and then settled on the rock, feet dangling out over the water several metres below. Alex folded his large frame down to sit beside her. 'What now?'

She sent him a wide-eyed stare. 'Why, we wait to catch a fish, of course.'

But he could sense her laughter bubbling just beneath the surface and it made him grin. It made him feel as if he was on holiday.

It made him feel young.

His grin, or whatever she saw in his face, made Kit's eyes widen. Her eyes dropped to his lips and he recognized the flare of temptation that flitted through them.

If she leaned forward and kissed him, he would kiss her back. Right or wrong, he would cup one hand around the back of her head, slant his lips over hers and explore every millimetre of those delectable lips of hers. Slowly. Thoroughly.

They were both holding fishing rods. How much trouble could one little kiss cause…in public, on a breakwater?

He glanced down at the oyster-encrusted rocks below

and found his answer. It took every ounce of strength he had, but he turned his eyes seaward. 'What are we hoping to catch?'

'Who cares?'

Her voice came out all breathy. Alex's hands tightened on his rod. He kept his gaze doggedly out to sea, but from the corner of his eye he could see the way she swung her legs.

'I am wearing my swimming togs under this dress, you know?'

'What?'

'You seem very disapproving. You think my dress is too short, don't you?'

'No, I—'

He broke off. He could hardly explain the reason he kept staring was because he couldn't help it, because she fascinated him, because he wanted her. *That* wouldn't help either of them.

'Bream,' she said. 'A couple of bream would be nice. Or whiting. They taste great—sweet and juicy. Lots of bones, though. A flathead, maybe? Just try and avoid hooking a grey nurse shark. It'll snap the line.'

'I'll do my best,' he managed.

'It'd be nice if the tailor started to chop.'

He didn't know what that meant. No doubt if he hung around long enough he'd find out. If he stayed.

Sitting here now beside Kit, that was easy to imagine.

'Oh, but it's good to be back.'

He turned to find she'd tilted her face to the sun— pleasure, gratitude and satisfaction all alive in her face. His gut clenched. He tried to remember her in one of her prim dark suits. He could—with remarkable alacrity— but... 'You belong here.'

Not that he'd ever considered her out of place in the city,

but here…she was home. Had he really intended to drag her away? How did a measly job compete with all this?

'What?' she teased. 'On a breakwater, fishing?'

'You bet.'

She adjusted her line…somehow. Alex just let his be and hoped it was doing what it should be. 'It sure beats the rush and bustle of the city, don't you think?'

He didn't answer. She was right, but he didn't answer.

'I was lucky to grow up around here.'

Her child would be too.

'Did you grow up in Sydney?'

'Yes.'

'Whereabouts? North, south, east or west?'

His stomach tightened. He didn't like talking about his childhood. But her question, it was innocent, innocuous. 'In the western suburbs until I was twelve and then Vaucluse.'

She spun on her rock. He shot an arm out to steady her. 'You grew up in Vaucluse—as in on the harbour—and you've never been fishing?'

'Would you eat what came out of the harbour?'

She pursed her lips, then nodded. 'Good point.'

He removed his arm from around her waist. He couldn't stay here in this golden place near this golden woman. Eventually everything he touched turned to ash.

He wouldn't do that to Kit.

In the next instant he nearly fell off the rock. 'Holy crap!' The fishing rod had developed a mind of its own.

Kit started laughing so hard tears filled the creases at the corners of her eyes. 'Reel in! Reel in!' she finally managed to choke out. 'You've hooked a fish, you landlubber.'

'A fish?'

He promptly set about reeling it in.

'Ooh, it's a big one!' Kit gave him instructions—"Play

the line out a bit, don't lose it on the rocks'. Frankly, he didn't have much of a clue what she meant, but finally he had the fish, flapping on the end of his line, clear of the water.

Jumping to her feet and bracing herself against his shoulder, Kit scooped the net beneath the fish and presented it to him. 'Your first fish!'

He leapt to his feet. His first—

'A bream! Congratulations, Alex.' With that she leaned forward and planted a kiss on his cheek.

He promptly felt ten feet tall. He leant in and kissed her full on the mouth.

She kissed him back.

They drew away and stared at each other. Her eyes were golden with sunshine and fun. Her lips…

The all-consuming need that had been building in him for the last fortnight broke through his control. He had to have more! Before he could think the better of it, he grasped her chin in his free hand and slanted his mouth fully over hers.

She tasted of salt and choc-chip cookies and some memory from his past that he couldn't quite grasp.

His tongue traced the inside of her bottom lip, revelling in her velvet warmth. Maybe if he kissed her deeper, longer, more thoroughly, he'd remember that memory and—

Her tongue shyly stroked his and all conscious thought fled as their kisses deepened. Her hand fisted in his shirt to draw him closer. His fingers slanted around the curve of her scalp, sliding through the silk of her hair to angle her mouth so he could explore every exquisite millimetre of her delectable lips.

Four months! He'd ached for this for four months.

It was worth the wait.

For a moment he thought it might just be worth anything.

Finally, with a gasp, she dragged her mouth from his, rested her forehead against his cheek, her chest rising and falling as if she'd just run a race.

'Alex, you've got to warn a woman if you're going to kiss her like that.'

He was breathing so hard he couldn't speak.

'At least make sure she has two hands free to hold onto you.'

She was still holding the net full of fish. He took the net from her. 'Sorry, I got carried away by the moment.'

No, he wasn't. He wasn't the least bit sorry.

She stared up at him then, a frown in her eyes. 'I'm not sure we should be doing that.'

He blinked. He wanted to do a whole lot more than—

Hell! He snapped away from her.

Kit sighed and sat again. 'Don't fall off the rock, Alex. The current is fierce and I don't feel like diving in and saving you.'

When he sat back beside her she expertly unhooked the fish and popped it in the bucket. 'Okay, next lesson—how to bait the hook.'

He took his cue from her. She didn't want to talk about that kiss and he was damn sure he didn't want to either. It didn't mean anything. It *couldn't* mean anything.

They caught two bream apiece. Even given that kiss, the confusion it sent hurtling through him, Alex couldn't remember the last time he'd had so much fun. 'I have to hand it to you, Kit. This fishing gig was a good idea.'

He grinned when she said, 'I won't say I told you so.' They sat in companionable silence, their lines dangling in the water and the breeze playing across their faces. They swung their feet and breathed the invigorating salt tang that seasoned the air and listened to the cries of the seagulls. 'You know, I always dreamed that my dad would take me fishing like this.'

He glanced at her out of the corner of his eye. She hadn't mentioned her father before. 'He didn't?'

She snorted. 'He didn't know one end of a fishing rod from the other.'

Neither had he before today.

'When I told my grandma about that little dream, she took me fishing herself.'

'On this rock?' He couldn't get enough of her stories about her childhood.

She pointed back along the way they'd come. 'We dropped hand lines further along that way in the channel. A much safer spot for a child.'

'And?' He didn't know what he was waiting for. He rubbed the back of his neck. Would his child dream that one day its father would take it fishing too?

The thought unnerved him.

'And we didn't catch a thing, but we had the best time.' She laughed, the memory obviously a good one. 'Eventually my grandma and I graduated to this rock.' She patted it.

He stretched his neck first one way then the other. Kit's child would have her for its mother. It wouldn't miss out on anything. It wouldn't want for anything.

Except a father.

'Your childhood sounds idyllic. You were close to your family?' He wanted her surrounded by family who would look out for her, support her.

'My family is my mother and grandmother. I adore them both.'

His heart started to pound. 'And your father?'

A shadow passed over her face. He immediately regretted darkening her day. 'I'm sorry, I shouldn't have asked. It's none of my business.'

'No,' she said slowly. 'I think you should know about my father, Alex. It might help you understand where I'm coming from.'

He didn't need to know about her past to know that she was wonderful now. But he was happy to listen to anything she wanted to tell him.

'My parents never married. Their relationship was over long before I was born and my mother had me without any support from him.'

'You and your mum were happy?'

'Oh, yes, but when I started school and saw the other children with their daddies, I wanted one too. I started asking Mum a lot of questions, pestering her about my dad until she finally promised to track him down for me.'

He could imagine the younger Kit with her golden hair and her golden skin and her golden eyes. And her yearning. He swallowed. 'And?'

'And finally she did. I was so happy. He took me swimming and for ice cream. I got to introduce him to Caro and Denise and Alice and all my other friends.'

'And then?'

She shrugged. 'I saw him off and on until I was fifteen. He'd show up three or four times a year with a belated Christmas present, take me out for my birthday, that kind of thing.'

She fiddled with her fishing rod, resettled her hat on her head. Alex didn't move.

'I was a bit slow on the uptake. It took me a while to realize he didn't actually enjoy hanging out with me.'

Bile burned the back of his throat. 'Kit, I'm sorry. I—'

She waved his sympathy away. 'You know, I could've

accepted it if he'd made all those visits out of a sense of responsibility or duty, but…I caught Mum paying him.'

He frowned. He wanted her to turn and look at him, but her gaze remained on the swirling water below.

'My mother had been paying him, bribing him, to play father to me.'

Her voice was strangely impassive and it took a moment for the import of her words to hit him. When they did his hands threatened to snap his fishing rod in two. He'd have preferred to wrap them around her father's throat. The hide of the man!

'I never saw him again. I was pretty angry with my mother for a long time too.' She paused, pursed her lips. 'But now, with a baby of my own on the way, I understand my mother's actions so much more.' She glanced at him and then glanced away again. 'You see, Alex, I want my baby to have everything good in this world and that includes a father.'

Her words chilled him to the very centre of his being. 'Kit, I—'

'I know what you told me, Alex. I know you said you would not be a father to our baby.'

Our baby. He closed his eyes. It wasn't that he wouldn't, but that he *couldn't.*

'I would love to change your mind about that.'

'I—'

'No, just listen to what I have to say. I'm not asking you to respond. I just want you to hear what I have to say. Okay?'

His heart dropped to his knees. He managed a heavy nod.

'I know what it's like to yearn for a father with your whole being until everything else shrinks in importance.

Knowing how important it was to me, do you think I would purposely and consciously ever deny that to my child?'

She turned then and her golden eyes met his. 'I couldn't do it, Alex. I could never do what Jacqueline did. I could never deny my child its father.'

He closed his eyes, tried to block out all her goldenness and the spell she was threatening to weave about him.

'Like I said,' she continued, 'I'm not asking you to respond to any of this. It's just…'

He opened his eyes. He couldn't help it.

'The thing is, Alex, if you're using that as an excuse to avoid fatherhood then you're going to have to come up with another one because that one doesn't exist.'

A hole opened up inside his chest. 'I'm sorry your father did that to you, Kit. You can rest assured that I would never do that to your child.'

'No,' she whispered. 'You mean to hurt it in an entirely different way. At least I met my father and had a chance to know him and find out who he was. Even if he did disappoint me, at least it stopped me from building unrealistic fantasies around him.'

Was that what their child would do?

'Anyway—' Kit shook herself '—enough of all that for one day. Wanna learn how to clean and scale a fish?'

He tried to match her tone. 'How could I resist an offer like that?'

Her laugh could no longer lighten his heart. Her father's absence had left a hole in Kit's life, had left an indelible impression there that nothing could erase. Alex hadn't meant to do harm to anyone. But his actions had harmed Kit, and they would harm her unborn child's.

His child.

He dragged a hand down his face.

'So you're squeamish, huh?'

He pulled his hand away to find her attempting to demonstrate the correct way to gut a fish.

She cocked an eyebrow. 'Not going to throw up, are you?' Her half-grin robbed the words of their sting.

He wanted to lay himself at her feet and beg her to forgive him. For everything.

He didn't. Instead, he took all of the fish from her hands and, following her instructions, cleaned each and every one of them. It was the least he could do.

'Excellent.' She took the last fish, bundled up their things and made to leave their rock. 'I'll cook dinner tonight.'

'Hey, hold on a moment. You can't cook.' He took the net and the bucket from her hand and handed her the lightweight rod instead.

Her eyes danced. 'I said I *don't* cook. That doesn't mean I can't cook. And I can certainly do fish on the barbecue, jacket potatoes and a tossed salad.'

His mouth watered.

They walked back the length of the breakwater. Kit hummed, but Alex's mind churned. And then Kit halted mid-hum, and just stopped to stare.

At a mother and her baby swimming—floating—together in the shallows of the Rock Pool. A pre-toddler-sized baby. A little girl if the pink bathers and sunhat were anything to go by.

A little girl. Alex's thoughts tumbled to a halt. He couldn't drag his eyes from that baby. A great aching hole cracked open inside him.

'Cute, huh?' Kit whispered.

Yes!

Confusion, fear, desire all whipped through him. Kit's father had only visited Kit a few times a year. It had been enough for her until she'd discovered his betrayal. Could

Alex manage that kind of minimal contact—three or four visits a year?

He'd thought his staying away would be best for this child. Now he wasn't so sure. Kit's story had shaken him, left him stranded in uncertain territory with the ground shifting beneath his feet.

'Did you find out?' The question scraped out of his throat, unbidden. He hadn't meant to ask it. He hadn't known he'd wanted to ask it.

'Did I find out what?'

She continued to stare at the baby. Her face had gone soft, her lips curved upwards and her eyes shone. His heart pounded against the walls of his ribs. 'Did you find out the sex of the baby?'

She turned and smiled. 'No. I want it to be a surprise. But if you'd like to know I'm sure the doctor would tell you.'

Her smile, her words, they took his breath away. Perhaps she meant it. Perhaps she would let him be part of her baby's life.

He stared at the mother and baby in the shallows below and his arms started to ache with the longing for a child's weight. Three or four times a year, it wasn't much to ask. He remembered the smell of a baby. The newly washed, baby-powdered and slightly milky smell. The softness of a baby's skin. The surprising strength when a tiny hand gripped a finger.

Three or four times a year...

He scratched a hand back through his hair and then, without another word, he swung away and strode off towards the car.

CHAPTER NINE

'THE barbecue is ready to go.'

Kit's breath hitched, but she refused to turn from the bench where she tossed the salad. Alex—freshly showered—was making her heart beat just a little too hard. That was why she'd sent him outside to clean the barbecue plate.

'Is it lit?'

'Yes, ma'am.'

Her lips twitched at his mock subservience. She doubted Alex had a subservient bone in his body.

Nice body, though.

Oh, stop it!

She finished tossing the salad and wished her pulse would settle as easily. She tried to force her mind to mundane matters. Cooking, dinner, food.

Her mind refused. It wanted to dwell on Alex. On the breadth of his shoulders, the strength of his thighs. Thighs she'd had ample opportunity to examine when they'd been sitting on the breakwater.

She tried to resist glancing around at him. And failed. He met her gaze, moistened his lips. She wanted to groan. She wanted to reach up and wipe the tempting shine away.

That kiss on the breakwater…

Momentary lapse of concentration, her foot! It had been heaven.

And she'd love a repeat performance.

Her gaze zeroed in on those lips—lean, firm and magical. Alex cleared his throat. 'What can I do now?'

His voice came out hoarse. She wrenched her gaze away. Cooking, dinner, food, that was what she needed to concentrate on.

Food…um—she'd seasoned the fish with butter, lemon juice and fresh herbs before wrapping them in foil. They'd take no time at all to cook.

Dinner…um—she glanced at the stove. Jacket potatoes were nearly done. Salad was tossed.

Cooking…um—she lifted the platter of fish.

'You can get out of my way, for starters, because this master chef needs room to move.'

With a bow, Alex held the door open for her. Her heart galloped at the grin he sent her, flip-flopped and then galloped again. She did her best to ignore it. 'Could you bring that plate of corncobs with you?' She sent up a prayer of thanks that her voice actually worked.

After arranging the food on the barbecue, she glanced around her garden. The light was pink and gold and promised to last for another hour yet. A light breeze made the very top of the banksia sway every now and again. 'How about we eat out here?'

'A picnic?'

She wondered when Alex had last been on a picnic. She'd bet it was a long time ago. 'Freshly caught fish tastes better eaten out of doors.' Besides, he had sanded her two Cape Cod chairs and accompanying table and had painted them a crisp, clean white. They were crying out to be used.

'Tell me the first word that comes to your mind when I say "fishing"?'

She wanted Alex to relax this evening. She wanted him to have fun. And then she wanted to talk.

'Rocks,' he returned.

She had an immediate image of his legs dangling over her rock on the breakwater earlier. Strong thighs and—

'Mountains,' she returned.

'Himalayas.'

Good, no sexy images accompanied that word. She turned the fish. And in the same spirit… 'Yaks.'

'Yaks?'

Laughter burst out of him and Kit refused to question the way her shoulders lightened. 'Yeah, you know, big woolly animals with horns.' At least she thought they had horns.

'I know what a yak is.' His grin when it came was sudden and blinding. 'But in four steps we've jumped from fishing to yaks?'

Kit had to grin back. She physically couldn't help it. Besides, grinning wasn't against the rules. 'I'm trying to keep baby brain at bay. Caro has warned me that as soon as the baby is born, my brain will turn to mush. I thought word association games and the daily crossword might help counter its onset.'

'Right, smart move. Okay, here's one—picnic.'

'Ants.'

They both promptly stared down at the ground. 'No ants,' Kit finally said. 'C'mon, let's get this picnic on the road. The fish is nearly done.'

Ten minutes later they were settled in the chairs, plates balanced on knees, eating fish, potatoes, barbecued corn-cobs drenched in butter and salad.

'Heck, Kit, for someone who won't cook you've done a damn fine job.'

Kit licked butter from her fingers. 'I have, haven't I?'

But when she realized Alex followed the way her tongue caught the trickle of butter from the back of her hand, saw the way his eyes darkened, her stomach clenched. She grabbed a serviette and wiped her fingers instead. She left the rest of her corn untouched on her plate. Alex wrenched his gaze back to his plate.

The memory of their kiss burned between them.

That kiss, what did it mean? Alex hadn't planned on fatherhood, but it had found him anyway. He hadn't planned on any kind of romantic relationship either, but...

She refused to finish that thought.

She shifted on her chair. Could she blame pregnancy hormones for the way her heart crashed about in her chest whenever she locked eyes with Alex?

Her lips twisted as she speared a slice of cucumber. Not a chance. That was due to hormones she'd had long before she'd ever fallen pregnant.

'The fishing this afternoon, Kit, it was fun.'

'Yeah.' She smiled. 'I have so many great memories of sitting on my rock—fishing, dreaming, hanging out there with my friends or my mum and grandma. It reminds me of summer holidays and endless afternoons and laughter and all good things.'

He stopped eating to stare at her. 'I'm honoured you shared it with me.'

Regardless of what happened, she knew this afternoon would always be precious to her. And what she'd just said to Alex, all of that was true. 'Do you have a place like my rock?'

He cut into a potato, but he didn't eat it. 'No,' he finally said.

His face didn't shutter closed. She took that as a good sign. 'What did you like doing with your parents when you were young?' She swallowed as a different question occurred to her. 'Are your parents still alive?'

'They died when I was twelve. Car accident.'

There was no mistaking the closing up of his face now. Her heart burned. Her fingers shook and she had to lay her cutlery down. 'I'm sorry,' she whispered. 'That must've been awful.'

'Not your fault, Kit.'

His words, his half-shrug...the fact he ate a piece of fish—fish she'd cooked for him—gave her the courage to continue. 'Who did you live with afterwards?'

'My grandfather. He was as rich as Croesus and as bitter as battery acid.'

Uttered in a flat tone—fact with no emotion. Kit abandoned the rest of her food. 'That's when you moved to Vaucluse?'

He nodded.

The exclusive address hadn't shielded him from life's harsher realities. She could sense that much.

'He'd disowned my mother when she married my father. Apparently a motor mechanic wasn't good enough for the daughter of one of Australia's leading politicians.'

She shuddered. Alex's grandfather sounded controlling and vengeful. It wasn't the kind of home she'd ever want her child being sent to. 'If he disowned your mother, why did he take you in?'

'The papers got hold of the story, and to him appearances were everything.' His lips twisted into the mockery of a smile that made a chill creep up her arms. 'He had to at least be seen doing the right thing.' He threw off his smile with a shrug. 'I'd have been better off in a foster home.'

This was the man who'd raised Alex throughout his teenage years? More pieces of the puzzle fell into place. Kit wasn't prepared for the surge of anger that shot through her on Alex's behalf, though. The people who should've looked out for him, loved him—his grandfather, his ex-wife— they'd betrayed him utterly.

She didn't blame him for guarding his heart.

Her chest ached; her eyes ached. Did he have to keep guarding it against their baby, though?

'I left when I was sixteen. I found work as a builder's labourer.'

And he'd built an empire on his own. But that empire of his, it wouldn't have made up for all he'd lost when his parents died. With an effort, she swallowed back the lump in her throat. She was glad he'd given her a glimpse into his past, but she wanted tonight to be about happy memories. 'When they were alive, what did you like to do with your mum and dad?'

Enough light filtered into her garden for her to see that her question stumped him. She had a feeling that Alex had shut himself off from his past to protect himself from all the bad memories, but in the process he'd shut out all the good memories too.

'I…'

She could see that he struggled. 'Did your dad like to kick a ball around the garden with you? Did your mum make the best birthday cakes?'

One corner of his mouth kicked up. 'Mum couldn't bake to save her life.' He sat higher in his chair and grinned. It made him look younger, wiped all the cares from his face for a moment. It stole her breath. 'We used to play this strange cricket game with a tennis racquet and a ball.'

'We used to play that game on the beach!' She clapped her hands, absurdly pleased at this point of connection. 'We called it French cricket. Though I don't know how French it was.'

'On the weekends Dad would tinker with the car and he'd let me help. He taught me all the names of the tools.'

She could imagine a younger version of Alex—dark-haired and scrawny—handing his father tools, studying engine components in that serious, steady way of his. If they had a son, would he look like Alex? Share his mannerisms?

'Mum's favourite song was by the Bay City Rollers and she'd sing it all the time. Sometimes Dad and I would join in and…' he stilled with his fork halfway to his mouth '…we'd end up on the ground laughing. Mum would tickle me.' His grin suddenly widened. 'And Dad would always say that we were in for an early night.' He glanced at Kit, his eyes dancing. 'I now know what *that* was all about.'

'They sound like fun.' An ache stretched through her chest. 'They sound as if they loved each other very much.'

'I think they did.'

Don't go fooling yourself into thinking you can get that kind of happy ever after with Alex. If it weren't for the fact that she was pregnant, Alex would've left two weeks ago.

Without a backward glance.

He still might yet.

The only happy ever after she could hope for was Alex realizing that he could be a good father, that he would be there for her child. *Their* child.

'I did have a place!' He swung to her. 'A place like your rock. It was a tree in the back garden—a huge tree!'

She could tell he was talking about his garden in the western suburbs and not the one in Vaucluse.

'There was a particular branch I always sat on. It was the best place. Mum would bring me out drinks and biscuits. You're right, Kit, food out of doors does taste better.' He set his now empty plate on the table and glanced around her garden. 'You know, I like the idea of having a garden.'

Her breath caught. Enough to give up his penthouse apartment with its harbour views? She crossed her fingers. 'All kids should have a garden.' She tried to keep her voice casual, which was nearly impossible when this all mattered so much.

'Yeah.' Physically he was present, but she had a feeling he was a million miles away.

'Alex?'

'Hmm?'

'If you decided that you did want to be an active, involved father, what are the kinds of things you'd like to do with your child? Hypothetically speaking, of course.' She added the last in a rush. She didn't want to scare him off. She didn't want him clamming up again. She just wanted to plant the idea firmly—very firmly—into his mind.

'I...' He dragged a hand back through his hair, shrugged. 'The fishing this afternoon was fun.'

'Nuh-uh, I bags the fishing. You come up with your own activities, buster.'

He chuckled but she heard the strain behind it. He swung to her. 'Kit, I've by no means decided—'

'I know.' She refused let him finish, wouldn't let him talk himself out of the thought of becoming a father. She touched his arm. 'But will you promise me to at least consider the possibility? Just to...think about it?'

'Kit, I—'

He broke off and dragged a hand back through his hair. 'I'll think about it. But I'm not making any promises.'

'Thank you.'

He rose and took her now empty plate. 'Would you like some more?'

She shook her head.

'I'll get started on the dishes then.'

Kit watched him take their plates inside, her hand resting across her stomach, her fingers crossed.

Three days later Alex wasn't any closer to knowing if he could manage the kind of involvement Kit wanted from him.

Whenever he thought of that baby girl at the Rock Pool, though, a surge of longing cracked his chest wide open. Longing that had grown into a persistent ache.

He didn't know what it meant. He'd discounted children and family for ever.

But Kit was carrying *his* child. Could he just walk away?

He swallowed, remembering the first moment Chad had been placed in his arms and—

His mind shied away from the memory. Thinking about Chad, he couldn't do it. It hurt too much. Thinking about Chad made him want to throw his head back and howl.

He rolled his shoulders, shoved his thoughts aside. He hadn't signed up for any of this!

When he half-turned from the house to seize the crowbar Kit appeared at the very edge of his peripheral vision, sitting in her Cape Cod chair. She'd gone still, her fingers no longer flying across the keyboard of her laptop and suddenly he realized she'd ceased working to watch him. He swallowed and forced himself back to face the house. He pretended not to have noticed, told himself it didn't matter, pretended it didn't affect him.

Impossible! All the muscles in the lower half of his body bunched and hardened. Her gaze had the physical presence of a warm caress, like a soft finger tracing willing flesh.

He gritted his teeth and ordered himself to focus on the job at hand. Several weatherboards on her cottage needed replacing before he could paint. With crowbar primed, he started prising one off, steadily working his way along its length.

He'd wanted to refit the bathroom before he'd moved to the outside of Kit's house, but the hardware store was still awaiting delivery on the shower unit he'd ordered. The supplier was out of stock. He grimaced. He'd have to hide that particular bill from Kit when it arrived. The unit had cost a bomb and Kit would have a pink fit if she ever found out.

He set his jaw. The unit was top-of-the-line, non-slip, non-breakable glass, and easy-clean. The fibreglass base and interior meant no grouting. Kit had heaved a sigh of gratitude when he'd mentioned that particular fact. He figured she'd be busy enough with the baby when it came without adding a high-maintenance bathroom to her list of chores.

He wondered if she'd let him hire her a housekeeper or a cleaner.

She won't need a cleaner if you're around to help her.

If…?

The nails, rusted into the timber frame of the house, screeched as he worked the crowbar. Finally the weatherboard came free and he sidestepped it as it clattered to the ground.

If only he could sidestep other issues as easily.

From behind, he heard Kit's quick intake of breath. He glanced over his shoulder to find her gaze glued to his butt. She licked her lips, her eyes dark. She leant forward. He went hot, tight and rigid as rock.

He and Kit, they had chemistry. Maybe…

Her gaze lifted with a slowness and thoroughness that had him biting back an oath and fighting the desire to stride over there, drag her mouth up to his and have—

'Oh!'

He blinked. Kit stared at him, her cheeks a deep, dark pink. She swallowed convulsively and then jammed her canvas hat onto her head.

He swore. He tried to loosen his grip on the crowbar. Hanging out with Kit like this—it was murder! For Pete's sake, why had she taken to working outside anyway?

She'd said it was to enjoy the sun. He'd told her that she just enjoyed watching him slave away. His teeth ground together. He'd been joking.

It didn't feel like a joke any more.

He wiped his brow on his sleeve and let loose with another curse—low so she wouldn't hear it. Who was he kidding? He couldn't stay here in Tuncurry permanently. Kit deserved something more than he could ever offer. If he stayed here she would never get it.

What about the baby?

Could he...?

Yes!

His lips thinned. Probably not. He knew Kit was getting her hopes up—hopes that he would be some kind of father to her baby, a better father than hers had been. The thought of dashing those hopes made him want to throw up.

He swallowed back the bile. No throwing up.

No hiding from the facts either. Darkness threatened the edges of his consciousness. He let it in to swamp his soul, smother whatever hopes he dared to entertain. The man he'd had to become to survive his grandfather's rule was not the kind of man who could make marriage and family work. His brief and disastrous marriage had proved that. His grandfather's tyrannical bitterness had killed something essential in him. Something soft that was necessary to make relationships work. That was all there was to it.

If he made promises to Kit—stayed and tried to build a life with her—eventually she'd come to see him for who he really was.

And then she'd leave him, divorce him…and she'd take his child away.

He had to stay strong. Damage control—that was all he could do now.

'You must be ready for a break, Alex. You've barely stopped working all day.' Ice chinked invitingly in the jug on the table beside her. 'At least have a drink.'

'Just one more board to go,' he grunted, working the crowbar again. Tomorrow, with Frank's help, he'd replace these boards.

That would be one more job done. Kit's house would be one step closer to being ready.

And he'd be one step closer to leaving here.

He didn't turn as he spoke. He needed a few more minutes to find his composure, to make sure when he joined her he could resist the spell she threatened to weave around him.

No matter how hard she hoped and wished, she couldn't make him a better man—the man she needed for her child, the kind of man who could share her life. But the thought of the child growing inside her…

Every day the evidence hit him afresh in the shape of her gently rounded abdomen, her heavy breasts. *Every day.* It worried at him until he felt he had a blister on his soul.

Finally, he turned. Kit smiled, but her hand shook as she poured him a glass of fruit juice. He pressed his lips together hard. At certain moments she could make him believe this life could be his. She could make him forget what it had been like living with his grandfather, make him forget Jacqueline's betrayal.

She could make him forget that his heart had grown as cold and hard as his grandfather's.

It was dangerous forgetting those things.

It was dangerous believing in fairy tales.

He had to focus on what he had explicitly promised her—to get her house fixed. Nothing more.

Against his will, his eyes travelled to her stomach.

How hard would it be to be a part-time father? To see his child three or four times a year and make sure it had everything it needed?

To make sure Kit had what she needed?

He glanced up to find her watching him again. He swallowed and took the glass she held out, moving back a few steps. He didn't sit in the other chair arranged so cosily next to hers. He didn't want her sunshine-fresh scent beating at him. He wanted to keep a grasp on reality. He sure as hell didn't want the torture of being so near and not being allowed to touch her.

Would Kit mind if he did touch her, though?

He backed up another step. Perhaps not, but if he made love to her she'd think he was ready for all this…this domesticity. He didn't feel any readier for it than he had on the first day he'd stalked into her back garden.

That thought almost quelled his raging libido.

If he made love to Kit, she'd expect the works—marriage, kids and everything that went along with it. They couldn't unmake the baby they'd created, but he could prevent himself from compounding the mistake.

He surveyed her over the rim of his glass. When she realized he'd caught her out staring at him again, she sent him an abashed grin. 'I don't get it,' she confessed.

All his muscles were primed for flight. 'Get what?'

'For the eleven months that I worked for you, Alex,

you'd come into the office every day the epitome of the assured businessman…'

He relaxed a fraction. 'And?'

'Look, I understand your roots lie in manual labour, but…'

His gut clenched. 'But?' Jacqueline had hated that about him.

'But I don't understand how you can still be so comfortable and capable and *easy* with this kind of work.'

Her admiration—admiration she didn't even try to hide—made him stand a little taller. He drained his juice and then shrugged. 'It's like riding a bicycle.'

'Believe me, I'd wobble. I'd stay upright, but I'd wobble.'

She made it so easy to laugh.

'Top up?'

She held up the jug and, before he knew what he was about, he found himself ensconced in the other chair, sipping more juice. 'I have had some recent practice,' he found himself confessing. 'In Africa.'

She leaned forward. Her lips twitched. 'Did your cabin fall down or something?'

He tried to warn himself that this was how her enchantments started—teasing, fun, laughter. He promised to bring a halt to it soon and get back to work. 'How much would you laugh if I said yes?'

Her eyes danced. 'I'd bray like a hyena, but…' She suddenly sobered. 'I understand you did some aid work?'

It was hardly a question, more a statement, but he nodded anyway. 'How d'you know?'

'The rumour mill at Hallam's was full of it before I left.'

'I was part of a team that helped to build an orphanage.' When he'd read the brochure he'd hoped that building an orphanage would help him forget Kit. And that it would help allay some of the guilt raging through his soul.

She waved a finger at him. 'You might like to act all hard and self-contained, Alex Hallam, but I have your number, buddy.'

He went to correct her, to tell her he was hard and heartless and that she'd be wise not to forget it, but before he could get the words out she said, 'You're nothing but a great big mushroom.'

That threw him. 'Mushroom?'

She stared back at him in incomprehension for three beats, and then she chuckled. 'Oops, marshmallow. I meant to say marshmallow. Baby brain, I tell you.'

He grinned. 'Is this where I point out that hyenas don't bray?'

'Of course they do.'

She promptly gave her impression of a braying hyena and Alex almost fell out of his chair laughing. 'That's not a hyena, it's a donkey!'

'No, this is a donkey.'

When she gave her impression of a donkey, he lurched out of his chair to roar at full-stretch on the ground. When he opened his eyes again he found himself staring up at an elderly lady.

Her lips twitched as she stepped over him on still spry feet. 'So kind of you to vacate your chair for me, young man.'

'Hi, Grandma.'

Kit's grandmother! Alex shot to his feet and did his best to dust himself off.

'Alex, this is my grandmother, Patricia Rawlinson.'

'Pleased to meet you, Mrs Rawlinson.'

'It's Patti, dear.'

'Grandma, this is Alex Hallam.'

'Ahh...' Those piercing amber eyes—so like Kit's—turned to him again. 'So you're Alex. I've heard all about you.'

She said it exactly the same way Caro had on his first morning here. The collar of his polo shirt tightened around his throat. Was she going to threaten him with a meat cleaver too?

'I hope you mean to do the right thing by my grand-daughter and great-grandchild.'

'I...um...' All the fun and laughter Kit had created in the garden bare minutes ago fled now. He had a feeling 'doing right' meant more than fixing Kit's house up.

Those amber eyes gleamed and he didn't trust them. He didn't trust them any more than Caro's spitfire green. 'I'd eventually like to see you make an honest woman of my granddaughter.'

'Yeah, right.' Kit snorted. 'The way you let Granddad finally make an honest woman of you on Mum's twenty-first birthday.'

'I did say eventually, dear.'

Kit's grandmother hadn't married Kit's grandfather till...

Both Kit and her grandmother laughed at whatever they saw in his face. 'Relax, Alex,' Kit ordered, her smile wide enough to ease some of the tension in his shoulders. The woman was a witch! 'Grandma's just teasing.' She tossed her grandmother an affectionate grin. 'Behave, Gran.'

'You young ones always want to spoil my fun. Now, Kit, dear, can you explain those extraordinary noises you were making as I came around the side of the house?'

'I was trying to show Alex the difference between a hyena's bray and a donkey's bray.'

'Hyenas don't bray, Kit, dear, they laugh. So, how did you get on?'

'Only Alex can answer that.'

Two sets of identical eyes turned to him for confirmation. His lips finally twitched too. He found himself inclined to warm to Kit's grandmother for knowing the difference between a laugh and a bray. And for having eyes identical to Kit's. 'She got on perfectly.'

'Excellent.'

It struck him that when she'd been a younger woman, Patricia Rawlinson must've been very beautiful. She was still striking now and she had to be at least seventy. Still, his collar remained tight around his neck. Hypothetical walls threatened to close about him. He wanted out of this garden fast. 'I'll…um…go put the jug on.' No doubt they had loads to talk about. He edged towards the back door.

'Hold on a moment, young Alex.'

He almost tripped up a back step. He couldn't remember anyone ever calling him young Alex in his life.

'I'd like to invite you both to a luncheon next weekend.'

Kit groaned. Alex's eyebrow lifted. It wasn't the reaction he'd have expected from her. Images of meat cleavers rose in his mind. Patti might know the difference between brays and laughs, but he'd bet she had a whole lot in common with Caro too.

'What on earth is this one for?' Kit asked. 'And how much will it cost me?'

'This one is for breast cancer, dear. A gold coin donation is all that's required. And I'd appreciate it if you could bring a plate.'

Kit's eyes danced when they glanced at him. 'Alex has been threatening to give me cooking lessons.'

'Oh, darling, if he can cook, why bother learning?'

He'd have laughed if his collar hadn't pulled so tight.

'I'll definitely come to your luncheon. Alex will have

to be a maybe. It'll depend on whether any deliveries are scheduled for that day. We've had a couple of delays.'

His collar promptly loosened. Kit had given him an out.

A new sick kind of nausea filled him then instead. Maybe she didn't want him to go to this luncheon. Why on earth would she? He was going to let her down, wasn't he? Maybe subconsciously she sensed that?

'Can I ask Frank and Doreen along? And Caro?'

Of course she'd like to have her friends there. He rolled his shoulders. Maybe she'd let him tag along too if he helped her bake a cake?

For Pete's sake! It was only a stupid luncheon. What did he want with one of those?

'I saw Frank and Doreen out the front so I've invited them already. Caro and co are always welcome.'

Alex thrust himself through the back door, but not before he heard Patti ask, 'Alex does mean to put your house back together, doesn't he, dear?'

'I believe that's the plan.'

He closed the door and made safe his escape.

That night Alex dreamed he was searching through the endless rooms of that brooding mansion, searching for Chad again, the childish laughter always just out of reach.

And, just like the other times, he jerked awake, drenched in sweat and with Chad's name on his lips.

CHAPTER TEN

ALEX dunked his paintbrush into the can of paint and set about slapping it on the neatly sanded, newly primed weatherboards of Kit's cottage. White paint.

One corner of his mouth kicked up. She had chosen white for the main body of the house and blue for the window and door trims. She'd snorted when he'd presented her with an array of colour cards with exotic names like fresh linen, grey gum, desert sand and sage. 'I don't want any of that modern nonsense, Alex. I've always wanted a white house with a blue trim. Ever since I was a little girl. I'm not going to change my mind now.'

And she hadn't.

So he was painting her house white with a blue trim, and found he was enjoying himself.

Next week he'd paint the interior—white ceilings, cream walls. She wanted her house light and bright and airy. It was her house. He'd paint it any colour she wanted.

The new shower unit was due to arrive at the end of the week and then he could get to work on the bathroom. Once that was done, all that would be left was the nursery.

His gut clenched and his hand slowed. That would mean looking at baby stuff with Kit, wouldn't it? He could imagine her face going all soft and misty as she looked at cribs and little blankets and changing tables with colourful mobiles. He dunked his paintbrush in the can of paint again and concentrated on transferring it to the weatherboards. Maybe it wouldn't be so bad. Kit had a way of making just about anything fun.

Besides, all that baby stuff could be ridiculously expensive. He slapped paint on with renewed vigour. He had no intention of letting Kit pick up the tab for that.

Kit. The thought of her had images rising through him. His hand slowed, the paintbrush almost coming to a halt. Last night while he'd cooked dinner—a chore they'd taken in turns since the night of their fish barbecue—she'd laid stretched out full-length on one of the sofas watching TV. She'd reached for the remote on the table behind and the action had stretched her T-shirt tight, giving him an eyeful of her baby bulge—small, but unmistakable. And perfect.

He hadn't been able to look away, even when she'd returned to her former position.

Beneath her shirt she carried his baby.

He'd stumbled back into the kitchen, trying to decipher the emotions tumbling through him.

His first instinct had been denial. He couldn't get emotionally involved with this baby. He'd lost it all once before. He couldn't go through that again. His second thought had been...

Hope?

Alex swiped the sweat from his brow with his forearm and gave up all pretence of painting for the moment. The longer he stayed here with Kit the more it seemed possible that he could do what she wanted of him, be what she wanted—an involved father. The thought made his heart thud against his ribs again, just like it had last night.

He'd started telling himself that this time it would be different. As the child's biological father, he'd have rights.

Besides, Kit had more generosity in her little finger than Jacqueline had in her entire being.

Plans started racing through his mind. He could work in Sydney through the week and then shoot up here to Tuncurry for the weekends.

Better yet, he could relocate here. He set the paintbrush down and rested his hands on his knees, his mind racing even faster. Kit had said the tourism industry was booming. There'd be property development opportunities galore. He could set up an office in Forster that specialised in developing eco-tourist resorts.

And he could be a part of his child's life.

What about Kit?

All his plans slammed to a halt. He swallowed. He couldn't give Kit what she wanted, what she needed.

What happens when she meets someone who can?

Sweat beaded his top lip, gathered at his nape and trickled a path of ice down his back. Eventually Kit would meet someone and fall in love with them. She'd marry. And his child would have a stepfather. He tried to push back the darkness that threatened to swallow him whole. He rubbed a fist across his brow. Kit deserved to find someone, to be happy, but…

What then? What if she relocated to Perth or…or to America?

Why would this time be any different? Why should it all work out for him now?

Because he wanted it to?

A harsh laugh broke from a throat that ached. Grabbing the paintbrush, he forced himself back to work. He'd be a fool to get his hopes up.

The back door slammed, jerking him out from beneath the darkness stealing over him.

'Good to see Kit has you working so hard.'

He glanced down from his position on the scaffolding. Caro. Not holding a meat cleaver. 'Nice to see you too,' he drawled.

Kit emerged from the house with a tea tray. At her side trotted a dark-haired child of about four. A boy.

Alex froze.

He didn't know why the sight of the child rocked him, but it did. To his core. He'd seen other children, of course, since he'd lost Chad, but…

He hadn't talked to one, touched one.

His hand tightened around the paintbrush. Maybe it was the combination of a pregnant Kit and child.

Kit and child.

Kit and—

Chad would be about this child's age now.

The thought slammed into him from nowhere and the strength drained from his legs. He braced a hand against a weatherboard. In the back of his mind he was dimly aware that the board was wet. *Ignore the paint. Keep breathing.*

Paint from his brush dripped onto his trainer. He clenched the paintbrush as if it were his last grip on reality as he tried to push the memories of Chad away, deep down into the unexplored parts of himself where they couldn't torment him.

It didn't work. Questions pounded at him.

Would Chad be the same size and shape as the child at Kit's side? How tall would he be now? Had his hair darkened or grown lighter? The need to see Chad, to hold him, burst the straitjacket he normally kept it bound to, and for a moment darkness swirled all around him.

'Look, Mum, I'm helping Auntie Kit and I got the most important job—carrying the biscuits!'

'Not just any biscuits, but chocolate biscuits,' Caro said with what he guessed must be the appropriate amount of

admiration. Thankfully she turned the child towards the
outdoor chairs and table. 'And you're allowed to have one
just as soon as you set them down.'

'Alex, that looks great.'

Kit's voice, her appreciation, pushed some of the darkness away and helped him breathe again. He did his best
to ignore the childish patter behind him.

'Would you like some tea?'

He nodded and finally found his voice. 'I'll be down in
a minute.'

She turned to carry the tea tray to the table, and Alex
clenched his eyes shut and tried to control his breathing,
tried to block the images that rose up to torment him, taunt
him, remind him of all he'd lost.

Tonight he'd have that nightmare—the endless rooms
in that mansion, the childish laughter always out of reach.
Despair threatened his control. Some days he thought it
would take his sanity. With every ounce of strength he
possessed, he pushed it back, tamped it down. He couldn't
lose his mind. He had Kit's house to finish.

He gritted his teeth. The mundane *would* allay the nightmare. He opened his eyes, unclasped the paintbrush from
fingers that had started to cramp and did his best to wipe
the wet paint from his hand with a rag.

'What are you doing?'

That childish voice came from almost directly beneath
him. He stared at the weatherboards. *He could do this.*
He'd wrapped his heart in ice once before. He could halt
the thaw that Kit had somehow started and put it in deep
freeze once again. He would not think about Chad.

He dragged in a breath. He didn't turn around. 'I'm
painting your Auntie Kit's house.'

'My name is Davey.'

Another deep breath. 'Mine's Alex.'

'Are you Auntie Kit's boyfriend?'

The voice was even closer now, and the question made Alex blink. In another time, another place, he suspected it would've made him laugh. 'I'm her friend.'

'I'm going to marry her when I grow up.'

He had to hand it to the kid. He had great taste.

'Can I help?'

And then Davey's head appeared and Alex's heart lurched. Davey had climbed up the side of the scaffolding. What if he fell? 'Hold on a minute, Tiger.'

His heart cramped. He'd always called Chad Tiger. *Don't think about Chad!*

Alex forced himself to move. He vaulted to the ground and then seized Davey beneath the armpits to swing him down too. 'Your mum will come after me with a meat cleaver if you—'

He couldn't go on. He froze. Davey's solid weight, his warmth, the trusting way he stared at Alex with dark-fringed eyes that were the same brown as Chad's. All of it was imprinted on his memory. A low moan threatened to burst from his chest. Chad would weigh this much now too. He'd still be chubby-cheeked and chubby-legged like the last time Alex had seen him, held him, but he'd be taller. He'd probably be asking awkward question and—

Who was letting Chad help paint a house or sand a chair or let him hand them tools while they tuned a car?

Pictures of Chad flashed through his mind. Chad running towards him to welcome him home from work, arms outstretched. Chad with his head thrown back, gurgling with laughter as Alex swung him around and around. Chad nestled against Alex's chest, his breathing deep and even as he slept.

Alex started to shake.

'Alex?'

Kit came into view. He barely heard her over the rush in his ears. The cramp in his chest grew until he thought he might crack in two. He wanted to haul this child into his arms and hold him close. He wanted...

He thrust Davey into Kit's arms. 'I...I have to go.'

He lurched around the side of the house. He didn't stop at his car. He kept walking. Chad's name echoed in his heart with every step. At some point Kit's started up in there too.

Kit's heart burned when Alex disappeared around the side of the house. His white-lipped stare, his wild dark eyes, the way his hands had clenched, it had almost made her cry out.

Davey had reminded him of Chad! Oh, why hadn't she thought? She should have realized.

Her mouth went dry. But...Davey wasn't Chad. If Alex reacted this way to a child he wasn't related to, how would he react to his own child?

She swallowed back a sob, not wanting to frighten Davey.

Davey's bottom lip wobbled. 'I only wanted to help. Alex doesn't like me.'

'Of course he does, honey.' She pulled him in close for a hug before moving back towards Caro, unable to meet her friend's eye. 'Alex hasn't been feeling very well lately. I think he might be coming down with something.'

Caro raised an eyebrow, but Kit was grateful she didn't snort.

'Hey there, soldier!' Frank popped his head up over the fence. 'Want to come see the baby birds in the nest on my shed?'

Davey's face lit up. 'Can I, Mum? Can I go over to Uncle Frank's?'

'Okay.' Caro laughed and pointed a mock-threatening finger at Frank. 'But mind you don't feed him more than two biscuits. He's had two already.'

'Aye, aye, Captain!'

Caro contemplated Kit as Davey raced across next door. 'Why are you wasting your time on this man, Kit?'

Was she wasting her time? She folded herself into her chair, hunched down to rest her head against its wooden slats. Nausea and exhaustion pummelled her.

'I mean, you had to see the look on his face when he held Davey. Not even Blind Freddy could've missed that!'

She had. Shock, wonder and then pain—a dark, searing, tear-the-heart-out-of-your-chest pain.

And she'd wanted to help him. In that moment it hadn't mattered if he was going to stay or not. Nobody should be asked to endure that kind of pain on their own.

'Kit, do you really believe Alex can change? Come to terms with fatherhood? Be there for you and the baby?'

Kit moistened her lips and swallowed. 'I know if our positions were reversed, I'd be asking you these self-same questions. Caro, my head knows what you're saying. It's saying the same things.'

'But?'

But her heart was another matter entirely. It hit her then that she'd been so busy trying to reconcile Alex to the idea of fatherhood that she'd forgotten to protect herself. She'd left herself wide open. She'd fallen in love with him again.

If she'd ever fallen out of love with him in the first place.

What a mess!

She forced herself to state facts. 'You know he threw up when I told him I was pregnant. Right there in the azalea bushes.'

'Oh, honey.' Caro leaned across, clasped her hand. 'I'm sorry.'

Kit squeezed it back. 'But he took me to the medical clinic all the same and he looked after me until I was over the kidney infection. He knew he didn't have to stay, but he did and he never made me feel bad about it. Not once.'

'Just as well!'

'His parents died when he was twelve and he went to live with his mean old grandfather. You and me, we both missed our dads, but our childhoods were great.'

Caro shook her head, but she was smiling. 'You are such a soft touch.'

'Every time I've just about given up on him, I find out something that gives me hope again. You know, he hasn't had a proper holiday in nearly five years. He took leave the month before last and spent it doing aid work in Africa, helping to build an orphanage.'

She'd grilled him until he'd told her every single detail about it. She could still remember the way his eyes had shone.

'Not the actions of a man entirely beyond hope,' Caro finally agreed. 'But, honey, I'm so scared you're going to get hurt.'

Kit pulled in a breath. It was too late to go back now. 'I know having him here is a risk, but...' She leant towards her friend. 'There's too much at stake to just give up on him. He'll do what he considers his duty—pay child support and whatnot.' She flattened her hands over her burgeoning stomach and stared at it in wonder and gratitude. 'I want more than that for my baby, Caro. I love it so much already. If anything I do now can help Alex with his issues and embrace fatherhood, then...'

'Then you'll do it.'

'I have to,' she whispered, her throat thickening and her eyes stinging. 'I know I might fail. I know the odds aren't great.' After what she'd just witnessed, they might well be non-existent, but… 'I have to at least try. Otherwise, how will I ever be able to look my child in the eye when it asks me about its daddy?'

Caro didn't say anything for a moment. 'What about what you need, Kit?'

'The baby has to come first.'

'Sure it does, but it doesn't mean you're not allowed to have hopes and dreams for yourself too. You know I'd lay my life down for Davey, but it doesn't stop me hoping my white knight will turn up.'

With all her heart, Kit hoped that would happen for her friend.

'You love him, don't you?'

It was useless trying to hide from the truth. She gave a weary nod. 'I started falling for him the first time I laid eyes on him. If I believed in such things I'd have said we'd known each other in a past life. It just felt that…right.'

And then they'd made love. There had been no going back after that.

'Do you know how he feels about you?'

'I know he likes who I am.' She hesitated. 'I sometimes think he has me up on some stupid pedestal. And I know he's still attracted to me.' Her heart fluttered up into her throat. There was no denying she was attracted to him.

'But something is holding him back?'

'Yes.' Chad.

'Honey, if you can't get to the bottom of it, no one can. If and when you do, he'll be your slave for ever.'

Kit wished she shared her friend's confidence. 'And if I fail, you'll be there to help me pick up the pieces.'

'Just like you've always been there for me.'

'Caro, if Alex can't be my birth partner, will you do it?'

Caro leaned over and hugged her. 'I'd be honoured.'

* * *

Kit found Alex on her rock.

She didn't mean to. She hadn't gone looking for him. She'd just needed to get out of the house. She'd needed the fresh air and spring breeze to blow away the fears and worries crowding her mind.

She'd come here to her rock to remind herself of all the good things she'd still have in her life if Alex did leave. Just the thought of Alex leaving bleached the colour out of all that was good. She swallowed and settled one hand on her stomach. That wasn't true. If Alex left she'd still have her baby, and her baby was a very good thing. An amazing thing.

A miracle.

She'd give thanks for her baby every day.

She stared at the rigid lines of Alex's back and shoulders and clenched her hands. Why was he finding this so hard? Their baby wasn't Chad. Their situation was different. Sure, the prospect of a new baby was scary, but it was joyful and wonderful too. Or it would be if only he'd let it.

She blinked hard. She should leave him be. He obviously wanted privacy. Maybe her rock would help him find a measure of peace. She turned to leave, but he swung around as if some sixth sense had told him she was standing there.

'Oh…' The words dried in her throat as emotion, yearning, her love for him, all swelled up through her. 'I'm sorry,' she finally choked out. 'I didn't know you were here. I didn't mean to disturb you. I'll go.'

'No!' He leapt to his feet. 'This is your spot. *I'll* go.'

His vehemence, his evident desire to put her at her ease and to do what was right, made her smile. 'I'm happy to share. There's room enough for two.' There was room enough for an entire family, but she left that particular thought unsaid.

He shrugged. 'I'm game if you are.'

He moved forward and offered her his hand, helped her clamber down. He let her go again as soon as it was safe, and she immediately missed his sure strength, his warmth. She tried to make do with the sun-warmed rock instead.

She rested back on her hands and lifted her face to the sun. 'Summer is nearly here. I love summer.' When she glanced back at him, she found him staring out to sea. Her heart crashed and ached and burned. Was he wishing himself a million miles away?

Regardless of his sentiments, it couldn't be denied that this stay here at least agreed with him physically. His forearms and calves had grown tanned from the sun. His body, if it were possible, had grown harder and leaner.

She'd love to see him naked.

Oh!

She must've made some betraying noise because he turned to her. She waved a hand in front of her face as if shooing a fly.

'Look, I'm sorry. I know I freaked out back there earlier with Davey.'

That was one way of putting it.

'But all of a sudden he was up on that scaffolding with me and all I could think was, what if he fell? It'd be my fault.'

'No, it wouldn't. Caro and I should've been watching him more closely. I keep forgetting how quick he is.'

When he didn't say anything else, a weight settled in her stomach. She stared at the water flowing in the channel. If she fell in now she had a feeling she'd sink to the very bottom. 'Tell me about Chad.'

Every line of him stiffened. 'Why?'

She lifted one shoulder. 'Because I know that's who Davey reminded you of. He's such a big part of you even though he isn't in your life any more.' Alex didn't say anything. She swallowed. 'How old was he when he started to sleep through the night? Where did he take his first step?'

Alex's hands clenched to fists.

'What was his favourite toy?'

He swung to her, his face twisted. 'Talking about Chad, remembering him, whatever you think, Kit, it doesn't help.'

The hairs on her arms lifted and her heart raced. 'You're not the only one who is scared, you know?' she burst out, unable to keep the wobble from her voice.

He frowned then. 'You're scared?'

If she had the energy, she'd have smiled at his incredulity, if she could just get over the ache flattening her chest and stretching behind her eyes and pounding at her temples first. 'Dammit, Alex! Some days I'm terrified.'

She couldn't bear to look at him any more, knowing the distance that stretched between them. She stared down into the strong current that rippled down the channel as the tide came in, at the clean, clear water. Then blinked when a silver-grey shape lifted out of that water. 'Oh, look!' She pointed at the myriad of fins that surfaced. 'Dolphins.'

In the past it had never mattered what it was that she'd brooded about as she'd sat out here; when the dolphins arrived things never looked so bad.

From the way Alex leaned forward to get a better view, from the way his back unbent and his shoulder unhitched, she figured maybe they had the same effect on him.

'What are you scared about, Kit?'

'That I'll be a terrible mum. That I'll be impatient and yell a lot and that being home with a baby will be so intellectually and mind-bogglingly boring that I'll lose myself and blame the baby.'

'Oh.' The word broke from him softly as if he'd thought her above worrying about such things. As if the thought hadn't occurred to him that such things could worry her. 'I think you'll make a great mum. I don't think you'll get impatient or yell. You never did at work. I know you loved your job, but how much more will you love your baby?'

He had a point.

'As for this baby brain you talk about, you're doing the crossword and playing word games and I know you'll beat it. Maybe you could pick up some part-time work that will give you some down-time from the baby?'

She eyed him uncertainly. 'You don't think it's a mother's role to be with her baby twenty-four seven?'

'Nope.'

She let that idea sink in. 'I'm scared of other stuff too.'

'Like?'

'What if dirty nappies make me puke?'

'Keep a bucket by the changing table.'

That made her laugh. She sobered a moment later. 'I wonder how I'll cope with months of broken sleep. I wonder how I'll cope if I get sick again.'

'You have lots of friends all willing to help you out.'

'I know, but…' She wanted it to be him she shared all those things with—the difficulties and the joys of adjusting to a new baby.

He'd loved a child once. Didn't it mean he could love another one?

'But?'

'I know all those things, but it doesn't make the fear go away. I…I mean, the thought of the labour terrifies me.' She gulped when she realized what she'd said. She hadn't meant to reveal quite so much.

Turbulence raged in those dark eyes of his. 'Then why are you going through it?'

'Because the hope is greater than the fear.'

Something fluttered in her stomach—like a hiccup—only it didn't come from her.

'What is it?' Alex barked when she held herself suddenly stiff, all his energy focused on her. It almost threw her concentration. She loved watching his muscles bunch like that, his eyes narrow in readiness.

'Hold on…' She held up a hand. There! It happened again.

It was the baby!

'Oh, Alex, look!' She grabbed his hand and pressed it to her stomach.

'What am I—?'

She pressed his fingers more firmly to the spot where the hiccup feeling grew. 'Can you feel that?' Wonder filled her.

'What is it?' He frowned. 'Should I take you to the clinic?'

She laughed for the sheer joy of it. 'That's the baby, Alex. That's the baby kicking.'

For a moment she thought he meant to pull his hand away but, almost as if he couldn't help it, his fingers spread across her belly and gently pressed against her, sending darts of warmth shooting through her. 'The baby?' he whispered, almost as if he were afraid of waking it up.

'Uh-huh.' She nodded. 'Isn't it amazing?'

'Yes.' Then he frowned. 'Does it hurt?'

He would've pulled his hand away only she laid her hand on top of it to keep it there, to maintain this tenuous three-way connection—him, her and their baby. 'Not a bit. It feels…wonderful! I've been dying for this moment.' Her grin must stretch all the way across the channel to Forster.

His eyes widened. 'This is the first time?'

She couldn't get the grin off her face. 'The very first time.'

Alex's wonder made him look younger. The grooves either side of his mouth eased, the creases around his eyes relaxed and the darkness in his irises abated, his lips tilted up at the corners, and it all made Kit catch her breath.

Beneath her hand, his hand tensed. She dropped her gaze to stare at their two hands. Neither one of them moved, and in less than a heartbeat desire licked along her veins. She wanted to lift her gaze and memorize every line and feature of his face, the texture of his skin, while she could. Here on her rock. So she could have this memory for ever.

She didn't need to look up to do that, though. His every feature was already branded on her brain. She knew that dark stubble peppered his jaw. Alex needed to shave every day, but he'd skipped that chore this morning, eager to get started on the painting instead. Her palm itched to sample that roughness, her tongue burned to trace it, to taste it… to tease him.

Today he looked more like a disreputable pirate than a civilised businessman and a thrill coursed through her at the danger she sensed simmering just beneath the surface.

Finally obeying the silent command she sensed in him, she lifted her gaze to his. At the edge of his right eyebrow was a tiny nick, as if he'd once had a stitch there. She'd always meant to ask him about it, but her breath came in shallow gulps and her pulse had gone so erratic she didn't trust her voice not to give her away.

His eyes burned dark and hot as they travelled over her, and her soul sang at the possessiveness that transformed his features. No longer afraid of revealing her desire for him, she lowered her gaze to his lips. Need, hunger, thirst all speared into her. Her lips parted. Her eyes searched out his again, pleading with him to sate her need. If she couldn't taste him just one more time she thought she might die.

Something midway between a groan and a growl emerged from his throat. His hand tightened on her stomach. Her hand tightened over his. Yes! Oh, please, yes!

Still Alex held back, his eyes devouring her face as if he was picturing in vivid detail every caress he meant to place there. He didn't lift his hand from her abdomen and it felt like a promise. His fingers splayed, sending darts of need right into the core of her, making her tremble with the intensity of her desire.

His other hand came up to cup her face, his thumb traced the outline of her bottom lip, dipped into the moistness of her mouth, traced her lips again, moved back and forth over them as if to sensitize them to the utmost limit of their endurance before taking her to the next level with his lips and mouth and tongue.

She started to pant, wanted to beg him for his lips, his mouth, his tongue, but still his mouth didn't descend. With a low growl she flicked her tongue across his thumb. He stiffened as if electrified. She drew his thumb into her mouth, circled it with her tongue, suckled it until his eyes darkened to obsidian.

And then finally, slowly, inexorably, his head lowered and her blood started to sing. His body blocked out the sun and, as he moved closer and closer, all she could see was the light reflected in his eyes. His lips touched hers, moved over hers—surely, reverently, thoroughly—her eyes fluttered closed and, as the kiss deepened, light burst behind her eyelids. Every wonderful Christmas, every sun-drenched summer and visiting dolphin, every bright and beautiful thing that had ever existed in her life gained a new vitality in that kiss.

The need and the energy, it took her and Alex and

merged them into a sparkling, flaming oneness until, body and soul, she didn't know where she ended and Alex began. It was the kind of kiss to shape worlds and change lives. It shifted the foundations of her world and all she believed about herself.

The hope is greater than the fear.

For the first time where Alex was concerned, her hope was greater than her fear.

Alex eased away from Kit. He didn't know for how long they'd kissed. He barely knew which way was up. Very slowly he drew his hands away—one from her face, one from her stomach. He tried to stop his legs from jerking in reaction.

'Are you okay?'

Her voice came out soft and husky, as if he'd kissed all her breath away. Served her right for kissing his breath clean away too.

He nodded and cleared his throat. 'And you?'

'Oh, yes.'

She had stars in her eyes! No woman should look at him like that.

An imaginary noose pulled tight around his neck, and yet for a moment all he could see was the shine on her lips and he ached to sample them again.

'I'm…' He cleared his throat again. 'I'm sorry.'

'I'm not.'

'It can't happen again.'

'I'll be holding my breath till it does.'

He closed his eyes. He was in way over his head.

CHAPTER ELEVEN

THE phone rang. Alex stared at it and then down the hall-way towards the bathroom, where he doubted anything could be heard over the blast of Kit's hairdryer.

The phone rang again.

He opened his mouth to holler for Kit. He snapped it closed again. She wouldn't hear him. Or if she did she'd ask him to answer it for her.

He snatched it up, barked, 'Hello?' into the receiver.

He hated answering her phone. There would always be a strategic pause, like now, as the person on the other end of the line—one of the very many of Kit's community of friends—tried to weigh him up by the sound of his voice.

'Hello, I'm hoping to speak with Kit Mercer.'

Female. It wasn't a voice he recognized, but something about it made his shoulders loosen a fraction. 'I'll just get her for you. May I ask who's calling?'

'Candace Woodbury. I'm her mother.'

Kit's mother! His shoulders immediately clenched up twice as tight. 'Uh…right.' He headed down the hallway and knocked on the bathroom door. And then he gulped. He hoped Kit was decent.

'I'm sorry—' that pleasant voice purred down the line '—but I didn't catch your name.'

His teeth ground together for a moment. He unclenched them to mutter, 'Alex Hallam.'

'Ah…you're Alex.'

He grimaced and rolled his shoulders, knocked on the bathroom door again. Louder.

Muffled muttering came from behind it, then it was flung open and Kit stood there in a white terry-towelling robe that stopped short of her knees, her hair fluffed around her face. She literally glowed with that golden light he found almost irresistible. He wanted to reach out and cup her cheek, slip the robe from her shoulders and explore her new lush curves. He wanted to kiss her like he had on the breakwater the other day.

He wanted to please her. Pleasure her.

His jaw clenched. He had to remember all the reasons why that was such a bad idea.

'Is that for me?' she said, all sass and fire as if she was aware of the effect she had on him.

She raised an eyebrow and pointed downwards.

Did he have an erection? He'd done his best to quash—

The air left his lungs in a rush. She was pointing at the phone. He shoved it into her hands. 'It's your mother.' And then he fled.

It didn't prevent him from hearing the start of her conversation. 'Mum, I see you've met Alex. I think you scared him off.' And then the bathroom door closed and he was out in the living room again and could breathe. After a fashion.

Kit's mum hadn't scared him off. He stretched his neck to the right and then to the left. He dropped down onto a sofa. Who was he trying to kid? All of it—Kit's whole life—scared the heck out of him. Everyone here, they had expectations of him. He'd rather deal with the savage cut and thrust of a boardroom coup than Kit's family and friends.

He leant his elbows on his knees and rested his head in his hands. He didn't have a lot of friends to speak of. Loads of acquaintances, but not many friends. He had a couple of mates from his building trade days, another from university and one from school.

He'd been a loner as a kid—his grandfather had made sure of it. In the last two years, since Jacqueline and Chad had gone, he'd shut himself away, had thrown himself into work. It hit him now that he'd neglected those four friends of his. They'd rung, tried to arrange outings. He'd ignored them, cut them off. Kit would never do that to her friends. He lifted his head and steepled his hands beneath his chin. When he returned to Sydney he'd contact each of them and make arrangements to catch up, apologise.

He slumped back against the sofa, his lips twisting. He had more acquaintances, colleagues and associates than he could poke a stick at, but it wasn't like the community that surrounded Kit. To his untrained eye, it looked as if everyone in town had clamoured to welcome her home. From her old school friends, to her mother and grandmother's friends, to neighbours old and new and everyone in between. He hadn't known until he'd come here how important family and friends were to Kit.

She belonged here.

He'd never belonged anywhere.

But then he remembered sitting in a tree, his mother coming out with milk and biscuits, humming her song, and his father waltzing her around the back garden. He'd belonged once.

Could he belong again?

'Ready?'

Alex started. He'd been so lost in thought he hadn't noticed Kit enter the room. The vision of her stole his breath. She wore a loose cotton sundress that fell to just below her knees, leaving her glorious golden calves on display. The dress—indigo-blue dotted with tiny sprigs of white flowers—made the golden highlights in her hair and eyes gleam.

The dress scooped down in a low vee at the neckline, making him swallow. He told himself he was grateful she wore a little khaki three-quarter-sleeve jacket with it. He just knew that beneath that jacket the dress would have those tiny shoestring straps. Straps made for being pushed off glorious golden shoulders. Shoulders made for kissing and—

'Alex?'

High colour stained her cheekbones, but her chin hitched up as he continued to survey her. If he reached for her now she'd let him. They'd make glorious golden love.

And Kit would interpret that as a sign that he meant to stay, that he meant to stay and make a family with her and the baby. She'd give all of herself. She'd have every right to expect the same in return.

It didn't matter how much he hungered to lose himself in her softness, her promise; it didn't matter how much he ached to give her all her heart desired.

The hope is greater than the fear.

He didn't know if that was true for him. And until he'd worked it out, touching Kit and kissing her, that was off limits.

He shot to his feet and swung away.

'Alex?'

He heard the frown in her voice and forced himself to take another step away from her and her heavenly, beguiling scent. 'I was thinking my time might be better spent getting on with the painting than attending a tea party.'

'You made the cake so you have to come. It's the rules.'

'You can pretend you baked it.'

She snorted. 'Everyone who knows me would see through that lie in a millisecond. Anyway, my grandmother is expecting you and the luncheon is for charity. It'll only be for an hour or so. Grit your teeth, smile politely, eat cake and then it'll all be over. Oh, and pack your board shorts. I thought we might drop in for a swim at the ocean baths at Forster on our way home. It's supposed to get hot today.'

The rest of his argument died on his lips. He and Kit swimming together? He wouldn't risk it if it weren't in a public place.

But it was in a public place and it was too much to resist.

The retirement village was on the outskirts of Forster. It only took them ten minutes to drive there and, although they arrived on the dot at midday, the luncheon was already in full swing.

Ostensibly the event was supposed to take place in the community hall, but it had spilled out into the surrounding gardens. Kit dropped a two-dollar coin into the donation box before he could stop her. He pushed a twenty-dollar note through the slot. He'd tried to do it unobtrusively, but her gaze had flicked back at him, mouth open as if she meant to say something. She blinked and then she sent him a smile that warmed him to the soles of his feet.

'That was very generous.'

He shrugged. 'It's for charity.'

'Okay, let's find Grandma. We'll say hello, place the cake in her capable hands, make ourselves up plates of goodies and then find some people to talk to.'

He bit back a sigh. It had all sounded great up until that last bit. He'd rather find a cosy corner and settle down to flirt with her. Finding people to talk to, a crowd, was far more sensible. Safer.

There was still the promise of that swim later. He'd hold onto that while he gritted his teeth and made small talk.

'I've been meaning to say,' Kit said, 'that I like this new casual look of yours.'

He wore a pair of long, loose cargo shorts and a cotton T-shirt. The simple compliment took him off guard. He didn't know what to say. 'Can't paint in a suit,' he finally muttered. 'I'd look a bit stupid.'

Her laugh made him grin. He could do small talk for an hour or so. For Kit. He could do anything she wanted him to.

Can you be the man she needs you to be? Can you be a father for her baby?

He pushed the thought away. He wasn't ready to face those questions and all they implied yet.

Well, then, when?

He rolled his shoulders. Later. When he had her house finished and… He gulped. The house was almost finished. Another week or so and…

Soon. He'd have to answer those questions soon.

'Alex, it's lovely to see you again. I'm so glad you could make it.'

He latched onto the distraction. 'Nice to see you again, Mrs…uh…Patti,' he corrected at her glare.

'Thank you for the cake, dear. Now, head on over to the tables and grab yourselves some food before it's all gone.'

'No chance of that,' Alex said. 'You'll be eating this for a week!'

Patti touched his arm. 'Make sure my granddaughter

has something with lashings of fresh cream. It's good for the baby.'

Fresh cream? He frowned. He'd baked a simple sultana pound cake. He wished now that he'd baked something with lashings of cream, like a strawberry shortcake. Tomorrow he'd make Kit one of those. He liked to watch her eat. He'd like to watch her lick whipped cream from her fingers. He'd like to drop dollops of whipped cream onto her naked body and slowly lick—

Whoa!

He did his best to banish that image as he followed Kit. She pushed an unerring path through the crowd towards laden trestle tables groaning under the weight of luncheon goodies.

She glanced back at him over her shoulder. 'How d'you learn to bake anyway? I thought you said your mum couldn't bake to save her life.'

'I spent a lot of time in the kitchen when I lived at my grandfather's, watching the housekeeper. Some of it obviously rubbed off.'

She started filling two plates with sandwiches, cakes and slices. He scanned the table for something laden with whipped cream. He seized a chocolate éclair and popped it onto one of the plates. 'Your grandmother's orders,' he muttered at her raised eyebrow.

Her laugh made him grin. He couldn't help it. He should be doing his best to keep his distance until he'd worked out how he was going to deal with…everything. When he was with her, though, that resolution flew out of the window. She made it impossible.

'Did you like the housekeeper? Was she kind to you?'

He met her gaze and saw hope there—hope that he hadn't been completely alienated whilst at his grandfather's. He swallowed. 'Yes,' he lied.

He told himself it was only half a lie. The housekeeper had been kind. She'd taught him how to cook and had taken him under her wing. She'd ruffled his hair and wrapped an arm around his shoulders at least once a day—her every caress a treasure to a lonely boy's soul. Until his grandfather had found out about it and she'd been dismissed. After that, Alex had been banished from the kitchen. He hadn't tried making friends with any of the other staff.

'Here.' Kit pressed a laden plate into his hands. 'Follow me.'

He shook off the sombre memory and followed her.

The small talk wasn't the chore he'd dreaded. He found himself in a circle with four of Kit's male friends from school talking renovations and home maintenance. He took mental notes when they discussed the predominantly sandy soil compositions of the area and the best remedies. Kit's lawn could do with some serious TLC.

Eventually, however, the crowd and the chatter grew too much. He eased himself out of the hall and found a quiet spot in the garden, lowered himself to a rock that bordered a flower bed. The sun beat down overhead. Kit was right, the day would be warm, but a nearby tree fern provided filtered shade and kept him cool.

'Hello.'

Alex's gut clenched. He swallowed and turned. Davey stood nearby. He moistened suddenly dry lips. 'Hello,' he croaked back.

The little boy took a step closer and frowned. 'Don't you like me?'

Heck, where had that come from? Then he remembered his abrupt departure earlier in the week when he'd thrust the little kid into Kit's arms and had bolted. He hadn't meant to hurt the little guy's feelings. 'Sure I do.' He held out his still half-full plate as a peace offering. 'Want a cake?'

Davey's eyes brightened in an instant. He raced over and promptly settled himself on Alex's left thigh and helped himself to a cupcake. Alex clenched his jaw at the child's warm weight, the smell of him. He beat back the panic that threatened to rise up and smother him. Panic he couldn't explain. *This little guy—he wasn't Chad!*

Chad. His hand tightened around the plate until he thought it might break as he fought the urge to remove the child from his lap.

Normal. Act normal.

He fought for control, fought to find his voice. 'Comfortable?' he drawled.

Davey nodded, oblivious to Alex's discomfort. 'I'm not supposed to get dirty,' he confided. 'If I sit on the ground I'll get dirty.'

Fair enough. He held the plate out to Davey again once the cupcake was gone. 'I hear the caramel slice is very good.'

Davey ignored him and reached for a piece of coconut ice instead. Alex considered eating the caramel slice himself—to give him something to do with his hands, in an attempt to occupy his mind with something other than the smell and feel of warm child—but he doubted his stomach would deal with food at the moment.

Given the choice, what would Chad have chosen—caramel slice or coconut ice? Grief as raw and hard as it had been two years ago sliced through him now. He set the plate on the ground, aghast at how his hand shook.

'Can I tell you a secret?'

Alex nodded. It was all he was capable of.

'Auntie Kit is having a baby. Did you know?'

'Yes.' The word croaked out of him.

'Well, I heard her and Mum talking and if she has a boy she wants to call him Jacob and Mum thinks that's a great name but there's a Jacob at my pre-school and he picks his nose and…'

The rest of the childish patter was lost to him.

The day darkened. He clenched his fingers into the soil of the garden, held on tight with both hands as the earth turned all the way over. He dragged in a breath and fought to remain upright. He would not be sick!

It came to him then, the answers to the questions he'd so desperately put off answering.

He couldn't do this.

He wanted to get up and run. Who was he trying to kid? He couldn't do any of this. He could not be the father Kit so desperately wanted for her child.

Any child, every child, reminded him of Chad, had memories threatening to burst forth—memories and pain. Davey, here, and…and Kit's baby, would act as constant reminders of his loss, would have panic rising through him…and grief.

Not to mention anger. How could he be a proper father to Kit's child when he couldn't see past Chad?

Ice trickled across his scalp and down his spine. He couldn't. The bottom line was that he couldn't.

Was this how his grandfather had felt when Alex's mother had left? Was that why he hadn't been able to show softness and love to his grandson? The way Alex now knew he couldn't show softness and love to his own child?

It would've been better for all of them—but especially for Kit—if he'd left that first day when she'd told him to. It would've been better for her if she'd never clapped eyes on him.

'…anyway, I think it's a dumb name, don't you?'

Eyes the same colour as Chad's lifted to his. It didn't

make any difference telling himself that ninety per cent of the population had brown eyes. At this moment in time they were the spitting image of the child's he'd loved and lost.

'What would you call a baby boy?'

Chad. He'd chosen Chad.

Davey frowned. 'Are you feeling sick again?'

Alex latched onto the excuse. He didn't know what the *again* was about, but… 'Uh-huh.' He glanced down at the child in his lap, blinked to clear his vision. 'Do you think your mum would give Auntie Kit a lift home?'

Davey nodded.

'Can you tell them that I went home because I was feeling sick?'

Davey nodded and jumped up. He raced off.

With a heart that grew colder with every step, Alex made his way back to the car.

Kit found Alex sitting at the dining table when she let herself into the house. Her heart slowed and relief flooded her. Alex did not look as if he were on his deathbed yet. Davey had exaggerated.

So…something had spooked him? Again? Davey?

She fought the exhaustion that threatened to settle over her. She recalled their kiss at the breakwater. She wasn't ready to give up on Alex yet. He'd make it. He just needed…

More time?

She swallowed. How much longer did she mean to keep making excuses for him?

He's worth fighting for, the voice of her secret self whispered.

He was. Her every instinct told her so. He worked hard,

he tried to do what was right, and when he kissed her she grew wings.

The expression that stretched through his eyes when he lifted his head to meet her gaze had a lump welling in her throat. She couldn't keep this up, not for much longer. At her last doctor's visit, her obstetrician had warned her that her blood pressure was creeping up.

Kit knew why. Alex. Her constant worry whether he would accept their baby into his life. Her constant worry whether he could overcome his demons. It was starting to take its toll. He was worth fighting for, but not at the expense of their baby's health.

Just give him one more week.

For a moment tears made his face blur. She swallowed and blinked hard. She couldn't find a smile and she didn't try. 'I see you've made a miraculous recovery.'

He shook his head. 'I'm sorry, Kit, I can't do this. I can't be what you want me to be. I cannot be a father to your baby.'

Her hands clenched, her stomach tightened. 'You don't need to make a decision about that right now. We can talk about it and—'

'No!'

The word snarled out of him. All the hairs on her arms lifted. The skin at her nape and her temples chilled.

'Every child reminds me of Chad. Every child is a source of pain. Remembering Chad every single day, remembering what it was like to lose him, it will drive me insane, Kit.'

His eyes dropped to her stomach and all she could do was stare at the white lines that slashed deep on either side of his mouth. Lines that spoke of grief and pain beyond her understanding.

'That's why I can't be a father to your child.'

For a moment, everything stilled, hung suspended—him, her, those words with their awful meaning. Then her stomach fell and fell and kept falling. She couldn't move, couldn't speak.

He'd warned her, he'd tried to tell her, he hadn't made her any promises. For the moment, though, it was his pain that touched her and not her own. She forced herself forward, sat in the chair opposite. 'Tell me about Chad,' she pleaded.

The darkness in his eyes didn't abate. He shook his head. 'There's no point.'

She reached out to touch the back of one of his clenched fists. 'There is a point, Alex, it's—'

'I can't!' he burst out, pulling his hand away.

She didn't know how one moved on after they lost a child, where one found the strength to pick up the pieces. Already she'd do anything to protect her baby and it wasn't even born yet. Chad might not be dead, but he'd been removed from Alex's world as surely as if he were.

She swallowed. She might not know what Alex was going through, but she did know that bottling it up would only hurt him more.

'You don't understand, Kit. This life of yours—the same life my parents led—it can never be my life. I don't have the openness of heart for it. I don't have any confidence in its permanence. If I stayed here with you and the baby I would ruin it all. I'm like my grandfather.'

'No, you're not!'

How could he believe that? She searched her mind for something that would prove him wrong. 'Look at how you were with Davey that day you were painting. He brought back memories of Chad, but you weren't unkind to him. What would your grandfather have done—yelled at him and frightened him, that's what.'

Alex shook his head. 'That doesn't change the fact that to survive living in my grandfather's house I had to kill off something in my nature that makes it impossible for me to…to do all this.' He waved a hand to indicate the interior of her house.

'You did it with Jacqueline.'

'If I'd done it successfully, she would never have left!'

For a moment Kit couldn't catch her breath.

Alex slumped. His eyes turned black. 'I will finish the work on your house, Kit. After that, I'll return to Sydney. My solicitors will arrange child support payments.'

Panic launched through her in a series of half-formed phrases and pulsing nausea. She surged to her feet. 'You can't leave just like that, Alex! I'm sorry, more sorry than I can say about Chad, but…' She gripped the air, searching for the words that would make him see sense. Words that would make him stay. 'Don't you see? Our baby deserves a father too.'

Alex rose. He stood wooden and stiff in front of her. He looked like a man who'd been dealt a body blow. 'I'm sorry, Kit.'

She reeled away from him as comprehension cleared the fog and confusion from her mind. Fear settled in its place. She swung back. 'You're doing with Chad what you did with your parents—blocking out every memory, good and bad, in an attempt to block out the pain. You think by avoiding those memories you're protecting yourself, but you're wrong. The same goes for love and family and commitment. Doing your best to avoid those things just means you're going to keep losing and losing.' Couldn't he understand that? Her heart ached and ached for him, and it ached for their unborn child.

She lifted her chin. 'I know you care about me.'

Please, *please*, don't let her be wrong about that.

Colour stained his cheekbones a dark, deep red. Hope washed through her. 'Walking away from all of this...' she lifted her arms out in an attempt to encompass the house, the life they could have here '...can you honestly tell me that's going to be easy?'

'It won't be easy.' His voice was pitched low but she caught every word. 'It won't be gut-wrenchingly impossible either. It won't be tear-your-heart-right-out-of-your-chest bad.'

She understood then the pain he'd suffered in missing his son.

'It will be for me,' she whispered.

Alex nearly caved in then. Kit's admission was a knife to his heart.

He'd never meant to hurt her. He'd do anything to take away her pain, but staying...that was out of the question. It was better to hurt her now than hurt her more later.

He should never have married Jacqueline. He knew that now. He'd worked long hours, driven to provide Jacqui with all the nice things she'd wanted—the big house, the antique furniture. She'd grown bored and restless, though, in all those long hours he'd spent away from her. She'd become lonely.

She hadn't been a bad person. She'd lied to him, and it had been a terrible lie, but she'd been too afraid to tell him the truth. If he'd put as much effort and time into his marriage as he had into making a name for himself in the business world...

But he hadn't. The harsh bitterness he'd suffered at his grandfather's hands had leached into his own soul. He couldn't do family. He didn't know how.

Unbidden, that image of his father waltzing his mother around their back garden rose in his mind.

With a swift shake of his head, he banished it. That was a lost dream. He wouldn't hurt Kit by making the same mistake twice.

Kit gulped. He wanted to pull her into his arms and let her sob the worst of her pain into his shoulder. He hardened his heart. She had her family and her friends. She didn't need him. She would be better off without him.

'You really aren't going to change your mind, are you?' Her voice wobbled but she held his gaze.

He shook his head. 'I'm sorry, Kit, for everything, but I'm not going to change my mind.'

'Then I was wrong,' she said slowly. 'You didn't love me after all. You don't really care about me or the baby. All this—' she gestured to the house '—has simply been a salve for your conscience.'

Her eyes suddenly spat fire. 'Get out, Alex! Just pack your things and get out. It's not our job to make you feel better for leaving.'

She was right. He should never have stayed here. 'I'll book into a hotel. I'll be back in the morning to keep working on the house.' It should only take a couple of days to finish the painting and another week tops to do the bathroom.

'No.'

She didn't yell, but the word echoed in his ears as if she had.

'If you don't mean to hang around for ever then you needn't think you can hang around for another week or two.'

But there was still so much to do! He couldn't leave her house in this state.

'In fact I never want to see you again. End of story,' she added when he opened his mouth.

'But—'

'Do you mean to stay for ever?'

He couldn't!

Kit gathered up her handbag. 'I'm going out. You have two hours. I want you gone by the time I get back.'

'Kit!' He surged forward as she made for the door. 'Will you let me know if you need anything or—?'

'No.' Her face had shuttered closed, all her golden goodness shut off from him. 'If you want to make things as easy as you can for me, you will go and not come back.' She paused at the door. 'Go home, Alex.' And then she walked through it.

His world split apart then and there. He turned and stumbled for the hallway and the spare bedroom.

'Alex?'

He turned to find her framed in the doorway again.

'Knowing all that you know now, would you give up those two years with Chad?'

He stared at her and didn't know how to answer.

'Understand that when you walk away from me and our child, that your answer is yes.'

With that she closed the door. And it was as if the sunshine had been bled out of his life.

CHAPTER TWELVE

WHEN Kit let herself into her house three hours later, she found that Alex hadn't left behind a single item, not one sign that he'd ever stayed here, ever been here.

She'd given him an extra hour to pack up, just in case.

She'd given herself an extra hour, just because.

Sitting on her rock for two hours, she'd stared out at the sea and had tried to make her mind blank. The cries of the seagulls, the shushing of the waves and the sight of the dolphins frolicking in the channel, none of it had been able to make her smile or had succeeded in unhitching the knot that tangled in her chest.

She dropped her handbag to the floor, lowered herself to the nearer of the two sofas, rested her head on its arm. When her watch had told her it was time to go home, she'd found she couldn't. She'd gone to a coffee shop and had sat over a pot of ginger and lemongrass tea. But the smell of coffee and cake and the chattering of the clientele, none of that had lifted her spirits or helped her feel connected again.

And now, back home and in the absence of the banging of hammers and the whirring and buzzing of power tools, the enormity of what she'd done sank in. *She'd sent Alex away.* And although none of his things remained in her house, although his absence was evident in the very stillness of the air, his presence was alive in every corner. His handiwork, evident in the freshly plastered and primed walls, mocked her.

And the deep malt scent of the man… She'd take that to her grave.

With a growl, she flew up and flung open every door and window. She seized a cushion and a throw rug and stormed out into the back garden to huddle down in one of the Cape Cod chairs—that Alex had sanded and painted. The day was warm but she was chilled to the bone. She wrapped the blanket about her and tried to stop her teeth from chattering.

A gulf opened up inside her, too big even for tears. Alex didn't want their baby. 'I'm sorry,' she whispered, rubbing one hand back and forth over her tummy. 'I'm so sorry.'

She closed her eyes and rested her head against the wooden slats behind. The sun still shone but it felt as if night had descended around her. Alex didn't want her. She'd always known that his rejection would hurt. She hadn't known it would devastate her.

She wrapped the blanket about her more tightly, knotted her hands in it as if it were the only thing anchoring her to this world.

Alex didn't leave town, he didn't return to Sydney like Kit had ordered him to. He'd meant to, because he hadn't known what else to do. *Go home, Alex.* Funny, but somewhere in the last few weeks Tuncurry had come to represent home in a way his apartment in Sydney never had.

When he'd reached the sign that said, 'Thank you for visiting our tidy town', he'd slammed on the brakes and pulled over to the verge, rhythmically pounding the palm of his left hand against the steering wheel.

There was still the matter of the shower unit. It still

hadn't arrived. How on earth would Kit be able to pay for it?

He'd turned the car around and had driven back into town, booked into a hotel. Not one of the gorgeous plush ones with glorious ocean or lake views. He didn't deserve one of those. His hotel was spare and spartan. His room was spare and spartan. His view… Who cared? He didn't bother looking out of the window.

Without kicking off even his shoes, he'd fallen back onto the bed to stare up at the ceiling.

Would you give up those two years with Chad?

He fisted his hands in the quilt in an attempt to combat the hollowness, the emptiness…and to give himself something to hold onto.

Alex was waiting for Frank at the Rock Pool before lunch the following Monday.

Frank didn't hesitate when he saw Alex; he trotted right on over and settled himself in the sand beside him. 'Saw your car was gone Saturday afternoon. Noticed it didn't come back Saturday night. Or yesterday. Or this morning.'

Alex was suddenly fiercely glad that Kit had a neighbour who took notice of such things, one who cared for her. It shamed him to think he'd written Frank off as a silly old duffer.

'Kit wanted me to leave. She ordered me to go back to Sydney.'

Shrewd eyes surveyed him. 'You haven't, though.'

'No.'

'You're going to stay and fight for her?'

Alex knew if he lied and said yes that he'd instantly win the older man's support, but he was through with those kinds of lies and half-truths and vain reaching for dreams that could never be. He stared out at the water. 'There isn't any hope for me and Kit, Frank.' The words tasted dry and vile in his mouth.

'Then what are you still doing here?'

'I can't leave her house in that mess. Not when she has a baby on the way.'

'Your baby.'

'Yes.' His baby. The baby he couldn't face. He pushed the thought away. This wasn't what he'd come here to discuss. 'Look, Frank, the short story is that Kit doesn't want to clap eyes on me again so I can't finish the work myself. I need someone capable to oversee the rest of what needs doing.' He hauled in a breath. 'I was hoping that person might be you.'

Frank pursed his lips. 'But I'd have to do it behind Kit's back?'

Alex nodded heavily. He'd known Frank would find the clandestine nature of his plan problematic.

'I don't know, Alex. Kit is a proud woman. She won't accept money or charity from me, and it certainly sounds as if she won't accept it from you.'

'Look, in terms of materials most of the stuff is already there. The paint is in the garden shed and the new bathroom tiles are being stored in the laundry cupboard. I'm not stupid enough to offer to cover the costs of the labour. I know Kit can manage that.'

'So…you just want me to oversee the work, see that they do a good job and don't rip her off?'

Alex nodded and pulled a business card from his pocket. 'The hardware store recommends these guys. Maybe you could point Kit in their direction.'

'That all seems harmless enough.' Those shrewd eyes surveyed him again, narrowed. 'And?'

'There's this damn shower unit I ordered.' Alex flung an arm out. 'It's top of the line, but they wouldn't take my money because they weren't sure if they could get it in. Now it appears they can and a bill will be enclosed upon delivery.'

'Ah…'

Realization dawned in Frank's eyes and Alex could read the denial forming there. 'It's expensive,' he rushed on. And then he named the price.

Frank's jaw dropped. 'You're spending how much on a shower cubicle?'

'It's top of the line—non-slip, safety glass and…and it's easy clean, low maintenance.' He dragged a hand down his face. 'I wanted Kit and the baby to have the best.'

Frank threw his head back then and started to laugh. Alex shifted on the sand and scowled at the water, at his feet…at a seagull that screeched endlessly nearby. 'You have to intercept that bill for me, Frank. Kit would never have chosen that unit and her resources won't stretch to covering it.'

'I'll see what I can do.' Frank chuckled before breaking into a fresh gale of laughter. 'Come on, lad. Let's go for a swim.'

Alex waited at the Rock Pool on Tuesday, but Frank didn't show. He knew Frank's routine was a swim before lunch on Mondays, Wednesdays and Fridays, but he waited there on Tuesday just in case Frank needed him for anything. Even though he'd given the older man his mobile phone number. And the address and phone number of his motel.

Frank showed on Wednesday. He told Alex that when he'd offered to organise for someone to finish the work on her house, Kit had accepted.

It should've taken a load off his mind. He knew this team would do a good job. But, as he and Frank swam, it was all Alex could do to keep afloat.

On Friday, Frank told him the painting should be finished by the close of business that day.

On the following Monday, Frank handed him the bill for the shower unit. 'Arrived on Saturday,' he said gruffly.

Not once did he tell Alex how Kit and the baby were doing—if she was eating well, if her last doctor's visit had gone without a hitch…if she was happy. He ached with the need to know, but he didn't ask. He appreciated all Frank had done and was continuing to do. He would not stretch the older man's loyalties any more than he already had.

'Guess once you pay that—' Frank nodded at the bill '—you can head back to Sydney.'

His words punched Alex in the gut. Leave? But…

'You've achieved what you set out to, Alex. Kit's house is coming along. The bathroom will be finished by the end of the week.'

So soon? Alex stuck out his jaw. 'I'm staying till it's completely finished. In case there are any snags.'

Frank opened his mouth but with a shake of his head he shut it. 'Let's go for a swim.'

'It's all done. Completely finished.'

Alex stared at Frank, a ball of heaviness growing in his chest. It was Friday. 'But…they said they didn't think they'd be finished till tomorrow.'

'They stayed late yesterday to finish up.'

The older man stretched his legs out in front of him. Alex couldn't stretch anything. He ground a fist into the sand.

'It looks grand.'

He was fiercely glad about that. He wanted Kit's house perfect. But finished…?

Was Frank sure? 'So the external painting is…?'

'White with blue trim.'

Just like Kit wanted. 'The guttering is replaced?'

'Tick.'

'The internal painting is all done?'

'It's lovely and fresh inside now.'

'And the bathroom is new and clean and functional?'

'Complete with that fancy shower unit.'

As each item was ticked off the list, Alex's heart grew heavier. He wanted to ask what Kit thought of it. Did she like it? 'What about the nursery?' He latched onto that as a last straw.

'She wants to decorate the nursery herself.'

She'd asked him to help her. His shoulders sagged. She didn't want his help any more. She didn't want to clap eyes on him ever again.

Not that he could blame her.

'So your job here is done.'

'I guess so.' The words emerged slowly, reluctantly. So why didn't it feel done?

'Did you know that Doreen and I lost a child?'

Alex swung around.

'It was a long time ago. Benji—he was nine. The sweetest little kid. Cancer.'

Alex stared. Finally he shook himself. 'Frank, I had no idea.' At least Chad was playing somewhere, happy, with his whole life to look forward to. 'Mate, I'm really sorry.'

Frank nodded. 'That kind of thing, it can tear your life apart, you know?'

He nodded. He knew.

'I'm ashamed to admit it, but I took to drinking for a while.'

Alex's lips twisted. 'They call it self-medication these days.'

Frank snorted. 'That's just rot!'

They both stared out at the golden curve of beach spread

out before them, at the clear water in the Rock Pool with its tiny waves breaking right on the shoreline. So calm, so peaceful, belying the swirl of emotions that slugged through Alex. 'What got you through it?' he finally asked.

'I had Doreen and three other kiddies, all who needed me. When I realized I was letting them down, I…' The older man's voice broke. Alex found his eyes burning. 'I suddenly realized that Benji, if he knew how I was behaving, he would've been ashamed of me.'

Alex raised his knees, rested his elbows on them and dropped his head to his hands. Sand from his hands ground against his forehead but he didn't care. He ached for Frank and for all the other man had been through, but their situations were not the same.

'You going to join me for one last swim, lad?'

Alex nodded and followed Frank down to the water. He grimaced at the term Frank had used—*last swim*. It sounded like a condemned man's last supper. When his feet hit the water he had to admit that it felt that way too. He didn't bother waiting for his body to adjust to the change of temperature. He dived straight in and started slicing through the water, pushing his body harder and faster. No matter how fast he went, his thoughts raced faster.

Kit's house was finished. There was nothing more he could do here. It was time to return to Sydney, or…

Or what? Stay holed up in his hotel room like some damn hideaway?

He kicked his legs harder, pumped his arms faster, did lap after lap along the net of the Rock Pool until eventually he thought his lungs would burst. Halting, he shook the water out of his eyes and dragged an agonised breath into his body. Frank stroked up and down not too far away.

Given Frank and Doreen's unrelenting cheerfulness, the way they were always eager for a chat, Alex would never have guessed that they had met with such tragedy in their lives.

Frank's voice sounded through him. *'I had Doreen and three other kiddies, all who needed me.'*

If his grandfather had taken Frank's attitude when Alex's mother had left home and married against his wishes instead of shoring himself up with bitterness and anger, he'd have gained a son-in-law and a grandchild who'd have loved him unconditionally. Instead, he died with all his wealth, but not a soul at his bedside.

Alex shook his head, turned to rest against the net and stare out towards the channel. He couldn't see Kit's rock from here, but—

He froze.

In his mind he'd just given his grandfather a choice. That same choice was open to him too.

His stomach rolled over and over as if he'd swallowed a gallon of saltwater. In his hurt, his grandfather had turned his back on the people he loved and had cut himself off. Frank had turned towards the people he loved. In providing them with the support and care—the love—that they needed, it had mended his heart.

He glanced at Frank and the message Kit had been trying to impart suddenly hit him. Love made a person stronger, not weaker. He pressed his thumb and forefinger to the bridge of his nose, his mind spinning. Turning away from love was the easy thing to do, but a real man didn't turn away from the people who needed him.

The knowledge poured into him, making him feel fuller and more real than he had in weeks. Than he had in two years.

Memories of Chad pounded through him—Chad, hot and grumpy from teething. Chad, tearing the Christmas wrapping from his presents one Christmas morning. Chad, completely absorbed watching a Labrador puppy. His chest cramped, a groan broke from him, but he didn't push the memories away. He readied himself for crashing waves of grief, but…

The pain didn't get any worse. It didn't take him over, bury him or send him mad. It didn't cover him in despair. And as he followed the memories as they flitted through his mind, he even found himself starting to smile. Chad had been a great little kid. He'd brought laughter and love and tenderness into all the lives he'd touched. Into Alex's life.

The answer to Kit's last question came to him bright and shining and full of promise then. He wouldn't give back a single moment he'd had with Chad. If he'd known that one day Chad would be whisked away from him, he'd have done all he could to have spent more time with him, not less.

He couldn't walk away from Kit and their baby. They needed him. They loved him. Such a gift should be treasured. He should be giving thanks for it every day, not walking away from it. He should be doing everything in his power to make them happy—to make them feel as loved and blessed as he was.

He swore and scrambled for the shore and then swung back to grab Frank. 'Frank, I've gotta go! I'll talk to you later, all right?'

'Rightio, lad.'

Alex turned and bolted for the shore. When he reached the beach he bolted towards the car park, half-falling in the soft sand in his haste. All he had to do now was convince Kit to take a chance on him. Again. He swallowed and hoped he hadn't stretched her love so far that it had snapped.

He hoped she would agree to see him.

* * *

'Kit!' Caro slammed her hands to her hips. 'Get down from there at once! Pregnant women should not climb ladders.'

Kit tried to find a grin, but from the expression on her friend's face it wasn't a very successful one. 'It's only a stepladder. I'm only on the second rung. I'm barely two feet off the ground.' She was trying to attach the wallpaper frieze to the wall. She'd thought decorating the nursery might lift her spirits.

She'd thought wrong.

The wallpaper frieze fluttered to the floor.

Decorating a nursery should be a joyous occasion. She hadn't found much occasion for joy since Alex had left, though.

She pushed the thought away. She'd made a pact with herself to stop thinking about Alex. So she forced herself to grin again at Caro. 'Ooh, look, pregnant woman on a stepladder! Must mean she's going to fall.' She gave a mock wobble, back-pedaling with her arms as if fighting to find her balance.

Caro rolled her eyes. 'In all the movies the woman only falls when the hero storms into the room, so he can catch her in his arms and kiss her.'

'Yeah, well, not going to happen here.' Her so-called hero had roared out of town so fast they hadn't seen him for dust. He hadn't phoned, he hadn't emailed, he hadn't nothing! She bit her lip. She had been pretty adamant, though, and for once it seemed that Alex had listened.

She thrust out her chin. Darn man!

'Jeez, Kit!' A large shape loomed in the doorway and her heart hammered all the way up into her throat. 'What the hell are you doing on a stepladder?'

Alex!

This time her wobble wasn't feigned. She recovered

herself and clambered down before she really did fall. She wouldn't let him catch her.

She couldn't let him touch her.

'What on earth are you doing here?' She wasn't dreaming, was she? She hadn't conjured him up through the sheer force of her longing?

But, as his dark malt scent hit her, she knew she wasn't dreaming. She wanted to cry. She'd just about rid her house of that scent.

'Alex?' She did all she could to make her voice hard and demanding, which was difficult given that she could hardly breathe.

He looked delightfully and deliciously adrift.

No! He wasn't delightfully and deliciously anything.

'Find me a meat cleaver,' Caro muttered.

Decision suddenly stamped itself all over his face. It took her breath away.

'Caro—' his hands descended to her friend's shoulders '—if I can't make this right I'll meat cleaver myself. You have my word on it. But until then—' he propelled Caro out of the door '—I need you to give me and Kit ten.'

'Kit?'

It hurt her to see him. It was wonderful too. 'It's okay.'

Caro shrugged and held her right hand up to her ear as if holding a phone. 'Call me.'

Kit swallowed and nodded. 'I will.'

Caro left before Alex could close the door on her. 'Leave the door open,' Kit said as Alex went to close it.

Shadows chased themselves across his face. 'So you can call for Caro?'

No, so she could breathe! His scent beat at her, making her light-headed. Not that she had any intention of confessing that.

She cursed her weakness for this man. And then had to

swallow at the baby's sudden activity. As if it too sensed Alex in the room and couldn't contain its excitement. The thought sent pain shooting through her heart.

She folded her arms and lifted her chin, stared at his throat. 'What are you doing here, Alex? As you can see, the work on the house is done.' Except for the nursery. And Alex wasn't interested in the nursery.

He wasn't interested in the baby.

He wasn't interested in her.

Finally, she lifted her eyes to his and her heart started to pound as loud and hard as their baby's kicks. The expression in his eyes, it said otherwise—that he *was* interested. Really, truly, seriously interested.

She swallowed, stuck out a hip. She'd been wrong about him before.

A ridiculous shyness, a ludicrous nervousness, made her hands shake and tangled her tongue.

'The house looks great.'

It did.

He suddenly frowned. 'May I have a look at the bathroom?'

She gestured for him to go right ahead. It was easier than saying anything. It provided her with an opportunity to feast her eyes on him as he surveyed the newly appointed bathroom.

'Do you like the shower unit?'

That unglued her tongue. She transferred her gaze from him to it and shook her head. 'It's the ugliest thing I've ever clapped eyes on, Alex.' Its fibreglass starkness seemed at odds with the rest of the room. 'What on earth were you thinking?'

'If it wasn't for that shower unit I wouldn't be here. It's that shower unit that's made me come to my senses.'

She pressed a hand to her forehead. The man had gone mad.

'And you. And Frank.'

She pulled her hand away, narrowed her eyes. Frank had been wonderful these past two weeks—solicitous and caring, offering her practical help but giving her space too when he sensed she needed it. The turncoat! He'd known Alex was here and he hadn't—

'He made me realize that running away from you and our child was the worst thing I could do.'

She promptly lowered the brand new lid of the toilet and sat before she fell. She covered her face with both hands. 'Alex, please don't do this to me. I can't stand it. Me and the baby, we don't want your guilt and your sense of duty and responsibility.' She got that, she really did, but... 'That's not what we need.'

'Tell me what you do need, Kit.'

His voice, its intensity, made her lift her head. 'We need your joy, Alex. We need your joy and your happiness, and we need your love.' She dragged in a breath that made her whole frame shake.

She closed her eyes and counted to three. When she opened them again, Alex was still there. She frowned. 'I know those things are not on offer. I understand that you don't have them to give. But please, don't torture me with consolation prizes. I...I can't stand it.'

He sat on the side of the bathtub so they were eye to eye. 'But what if they are on offer, Kit? What if I tell you I've found my joy, my happiness and my love? What if I tell you I've found all those things?' He reached over and flattened his hand against her baby bump. 'What if I tell you I know those things are here in this room with me? Kit, what if I tell you that you and our baby...'

She blinked. He'd said *our* baby. Not *her* baby or *the* baby but *our* baby!

'...that you are my joy and my happiness and my love?'

She gripped her hands together. The only thing keeping her steady was his hand on her baby bump. 'If you did by some miracle say those things to me, I'd say that you'd have a hard time convincing me of their truth.'

But his eyes, his smile, the light shining in his face and the way his hand curved against her stomach. All those things told her that he spoke the truth.

He leaned towards her. 'Frank told me about Benji.'

Her jaw went slack. That meant Frank trusted Alex. Really trusted him.

'And that's when I realized what you'd been trying to show me all along—that love isn't a weakness, it's a strength. And that's when I could finally answer that last question you asked me.'

He met her gaze—strong and steadfast. 'I would not give up a single moment I had with Chad.'

The truth shone from every inch of his being. Hope lifted through her. She tried to keep it in check while she took in the deeper meaning of his words.

'I don't want to waste a single moment of the time I'm given with you and our child either. It's too precious. I want to treasure it.'

He went down on one knee in front of her. Her hope burst free. 'Alex! You can't propose to me when I'm sitting on a toilet!'

His grin when it came was slow and sexy as all get out. 'Considering I stayed in town because of that darn shower unit, I think the bathroom is the perfect place to propose to you.'

She glanced at the shower unit.

'I'll explain it to you later,' he promised, taking her

hand. 'What I have to say now is much more important, believe me.'

Oh, she did. When he looked at her like that she'd believe anything.

'Kit, what happened with Jacqui and Chad, for a long time I thought that must have been my fault. I figured that if I'd been a better father and husband, they wouldn't have left like that.'

'Oh, Alex.' She cupped his face with her free hand.

'But I've started to realize it doesn't prove I'm either a bad husband or a bad father. I just wasn't the right husband for Jacqui. And, if I'm truly honest, she was never the right wife for me. It took a long time for me to realize that because I was so busy counting all the similarities between my grandfather and me. I thought his coldness and bitterness were part of my genetic make-up too. But my mother wasn't like that.

'There's no reason why I have to be like him either. He had choices too. He made the wrong choices.' His eyes didn't drop from hers, not once. 'I don't have to be like him unless I choose to be. And, Kit—' his grip tightened about her hand '—I'm choosing not to be.'

She still held his face cupped in her hand and she couldn't help herself, she leaned forward and pressed her lips to his.

He kissed her back—gently, wonderingly and with the same love that had splintered her mind when he'd kissed her at the breakwater that day.

He gripped her by the shoulders and pulled back. 'No way! No more of that.'

Her eyes bugged.

He smiled that slow, sexy grin. 'Until you tell me that you'll be my wife.' His expression sobered. 'Kit, I love you more than I ever dreamt it was possible to love another person. I will spend every single moment of every single day making you and our children happy. I swear.'

Her breath hitched. 'Children?'

'I hope so,' he murmured. 'You do want more children, don't you? We'd want brothers and sisters for junior here.'

Through a blur she desperately tried to blink away, she nodded. She wanted children, she wanted the life he'd described. She wanted him. 'I love you, Alex. You, this baby, this bathroom—' she suddenly laughed '—it's all I've ever wanted. Yes, I will marry you!'

With a whoop, Alex swung her up and around and kissed her till she could barely breathe. She wrapped her arms around his neck and kissed him back.

She didn't know how long they stayed like that. She only knew that it was quite some time—a wonderful, magical, I-can't-believe-this-is-happening time. Alex rested his forehead against hers. She swore she could stare into those dark eyes of his for all of time. 'Are you sure this is what you want?' she whispered. This had been such a hard road for him. If he needed more time…

'I've never been surer of anything in my life. I'm only sorry it took me so long to come to my senses. Knowing that I hurt you—'

'Shh.' She reached up to brush the frown from his brow. 'It's the future we look towards now, not the past.'

He seized her hand and pressed a kiss to her palm. 'Kit, I don't have much to offer you. I don't have any family and I've only a few friends…'

She smiled then. 'Alex, I don't think there's another billionaire on the planet who would ever say that they didn't have much to offer.' She took his hand then and pressed a kiss to his palm. 'I have enough friends and family for us both. We'll make our own family. Alex, all I want is your heart.'

'It's yours.'

She went to kiss him again and then stopped, cocked her head to one side. 'Can you hear that?'

'Hear what?' he said, nuzzling the side of her neck.

Mmm. She wrapped her arms around his neck and…

She cocked her head to the side again. 'Someone is singing in the back garden.'

He lifted his head. 'They are?'

She took his hand and led him through the house and all the way out to the back door and then stumbled to a halt as four sets of eyes swung to them—Caro, Frank, Doreen and Davey, who was singing.

'Well?' Caro demanded.

'Speak up, lad,' Frank ordered. 'Do we all get to dance at your wedding?'

Alex's grin threatened to split his face in two. Kit's breath caught. She'd never seen him look so happy. If she'd had any doubts left about his feelings for her, they'd be gone now. He glanced at her and she nodded.

He held his arms out. 'You're looking at the happiest man on the planet. Kit's agreed to marry me.'

Frank popped a bottle of champagne as Caro and Doreen swamped them in hugs.

'Ooh, I shouldn't,' Kit said when Doreen pressed a glass of champagne into her hand.

'Tsk! In my day it was considered healthful to take a glass of beer in the evenings. Never did any of us any harm. A thimbleful won't hurt you any.'

Doreen was right. Her doctor had said the same. A sip or two wouldn't hurt her. It was only right they celebrate the happiest day of her life.

'To Kit and Alex,' Frank boomed, raising his glass. 'Many congratulations!'

They all lifted their glasses—even Davey, who had a champagne flute full of lemonade—and drank.

Kit snagged Caro's arm. 'You will be my bridesmaid, won't you?'

'You bet!' She slanted a grin at Alex. 'The meat cleaver gets them every time.'

He laughed and kissed Caro's cheek. 'Had me shaking in my boots.'

Caro nearly spluttered champagne all over them. 'Liar!'

She sobered a moment later. 'Okay, so when are you going to have the wedding? Before or after the baby is born?'

'After,' Kit said at the same moment Alex said, 'Before.'

Caro grinned. 'Right, so you've discussed it then?'

Kit turned to Alex. 'I thought you might want some time to get used to the idea.'

'This isn't some *idea*, Kit. This is my life—our life.' He reached out and touched her face with sure fingers that made her breath quicken. His thumb trailed a path down to the corner of her mouth. 'I know what I want and that's you and the baby.'

She'd never seen him look more serious in all the time she'd known him. Her chest expanded and she could've sworn the only thing keeping her from floating off into the stratosphere and turning weightless somersaults was his hand on her face, with that maddening thumb brushing back and forth at the corner of her mouth. She reached up and seized it before it tempted her to do something that would make her blush.

'So…' She kept her eyes fixed on his. 'Before the baby, then? We'll get married before the baby is born?'

He nodded, his eyes intent. 'Yes.'

A smile built through her. 'In the first weekend Mum can make it down to give me away.'

'Am I rushing you?' He suddenly frowned. 'Weddings traditionally take a long time to organise, don't they?'

She didn't want him to frown; she wanted him smiling. 'I've never much cared about all the trappings that go along with a wedding. I'd be happy to have the ceremony here in the garden.'

'Won't fit,' Caro said, sipping her champagne.

'Lovey, you'd be better off at the community hall in your grandmother's retirement village. She can organise one of her luncheons for you.'

Kit glanced up at Alex. 'What do you think?'

'Does it mean you're going to marry me sooner rather than later?'

She grinned. 'It does.'

His lips descended to hers. 'Then it sounds perfect to me.'

'Mmm,' she murmured against his lips. *Perfect* was exactly how it sounded.

* * * * *

CLASSIC

Quintessential, modern love stories
that are romance at its finest.

COMING NEXT MONTH
AVAILABLE JANUARY 10, 2012

#4285 MASTER OF THE OUTBACK
Margaret Way

#4286 THE RELUCTANT PRINCESS
Raye Morgan

#4287 THE BALLERINA BRIDE
Once Upon a Kiss...
Fiona Harper

#4288 MARDIE AND THE CITY SURGEON
Banksia Bay
Marion Lennox

#4289 THE TYCOON WHO HEALED HER HEART
Melissa James

#4290 WHO WANTS TO MARRY A MILLIONAIRE?
Nicola Marsh

REQUEST YOUR FREE BOOKS!
2 FREE NOVELS PLUS 2 FREE GIFTS!

Harlequin®

Romance

From the Heart, For the Heart

YES! Please send me 2 FREE Harlequin® Romance novels and my 2 FREE gifts (gifts are worth about $10). After receiving them, if I don't wish to receive any more books, I can return the shipping statement marked "cancel". If I don't cancel, I will receive 6 brand-new novels every month and be billed just $4.09 per book in the U.S. or $4.49 per book in Canada. That's a savings of at least 14% off the cover price! It's quite a bargain! Shipping and handling is just 50¢ per book in the U.S. and 75¢ per book in Canada.* I understand that accepting the 2 free books and gifts places me under no obligation to buy anything. I can always return a shipment and cancel at any time. Even if I never buy another book, the two free books and gifts are mine to keep forever.

116/316 HDN FESE

Name _____ (PLEASE PRINT) _____

Address _____ Apt. # _____

City _____ State/Prov. _____ Zip/Postal Code _____

Signature (if under 18, a parent or guardian must sign)

Mail to the Reader Service:
IN U.S.A.: P.O. Box 1867, Buffalo, NY 14240-1867
IN CANADA: P.O. Box 609, Fort Erie, Ontario L2A 5X3

Not valid for current subscribers to Harlequin Romance books.

**Are you a subscriber to Harlequin Romance books
and want to receive the larger-print edition?
Call 1-800-873-8635 or visit www.ReaderService.com.**

* Terms and prices subject to change without notice. Prices do not include applicable taxes. Sales tax applicable in N.Y. Canadian residents will be charged applicable taxes. Offer not valid in Quebec. This offer is limited to one order per household. All orders subject to credit approval. Credit or debit balances in a customer's account(s) may be offset by any other outstanding balance owed by or to the customer. Please allow 4 to 6 weeks for delivery. Offer available while quantities last.

Your Privacy—The Reader Service is committed to protecting your privacy. Our Privacy Policy is available online at www.ReaderService.com or upon request from the Reader Service.

We make a portion of our mailing list available to reputable third parties that offer products we believe may interest you. If you prefer that we not exchange your name with third parties, or if you wish to clarify or modify your communication preferences, please visit us at www.ReaderService.com/consumerschoice or write to us at Reader Service Preference Service, P.O. Box 9062, Buffalo, NY 14269. Include your complete name and address.

HR11B

*Brittany Grayson survived a horrible ordeal at the hands
of a serial killer known as The Professional...
who's after her now?*

*Harlequin® Romantic Suspense presents a new installment
in Carla Cassidy's reader-favorite miniseries,*
LAWMEN OF BLACK ROCK.

Enjoy a sneak peek of
TOOL BELT DEFENDER.

*Available January 2012
from Harlequin® Romantic Suspense.*

"**B**rittany?" His voice was deep and pleasant and made
her realize she'd been staring at him openmouthed through
the screen door.

"Yes, I'm Brittany and you must be…" Her mind suddenly went blank.

"Alex. Alex Crawford, Chad's friend. You called him
about a deck?"

As she unlocked the screen, she realized she wasn't
quite ready yet to allow a stranger inside, especially a male
stranger.

"Yes, I did. It's nice to meet you, Alex. Let's walk around
back and I'll show you what I have in mind," she said. She
frowned as she realized there was no car in her driveway.
"Did you walk here?" she asked.

His eyes were a warm blue that stood out against his
tanned face and was complemented by his slightly shaggy
dark hair. "I live three doors up." He pointed up the street to
the Walker home that had been on the market for a while.

"How long have you lived there?"

"I moved in about six weeks ago," he replied as they

walked around the side of the house.

That explained why she didn't know the Walkers had moved out and Mr. Hard Body had moved in. Six weeks ago she'd still been living at her brother Benjamin's house trying to heal from the trauma she'd lived through.

As they reached the backyard she motioned toward the broken brick patio just outside the back door. "What I'd like is a wooden deck big enough to hold a barbecue pit and an umbrella table and, of course, lots of people."

He nodded and pulled a tape measure from his tool belt. "An outdoor entertainment area," he said.

"Exactly," she replied and watched as he began to walk the site. The last thing Brittany had wanted to think about over the past eight months of her life was men. But looking at Alex Crawford definitely gave her a slight flutter of pure feminine pleasure.

*Will Brittany be able to heal in the arms of Alex,
her hotter-than-sin handyman...or will a second
psychopath silence her forever? Find out in*
TOOL BELT DEFENDER
Available January 2012
from Harlequin® Romantic Suspense
wherever books are sold.